THE
PROPHECY

Peter W.E. Doidge.

July 1952.

THE PROPHECY

WILLY KRAMP

SCM PRESS LTD
56 BLOOMSBURY STREET
LONDON

First published in Great Britain, July 1952

Translated from the German Die Prophezeiung
(Deuerlische Verlagsbuchhandlung Göttingen)
by K. and R. Gregor Smith

Printed in Great Britain by
Northumberland Press Limited
Gateshead on Tyne

Chapter One

IN THE CAMP they were called the penguins.

There was, in fact, about the two Becklam brothers something of the sleek, pedantic complacency of penguins. It was this which marked them off from the rest of the prisoners of war, who in that first year behind the misery of barbed wire were distracted by hunger and a savage, impotent longing, and thus were more like wolves or foxes or some other evil and furtive creatures. The Becklams chanced to meet again in a White Russian camp: this meeting had been prophesied to one of them, along with other things which, he alleged, had come to pass in the same amazing way. The Becklams delighted to talk with a kind of ceremonious unction about the fulfilment of these prophecies. Hunched up on their planks at night, or waiting to be marched out of the gate in the morning in their clean field-grey coats, they were always surrounded by a little knot of men who almost gobbled the words from out of their mouths. For—as we shall see—the tales of the two brothers concerned the future of all the others in a strange and uncanny way. Many knew these marvellous events almost by heart; but this only made them the more avid to hear, like children who want to listen to a fairy-tale again and again, though they know every word. No wonder that the two story-tellers were in such harmony that they seemed to be one person and to speak with one voice. The one could take up the other's words in the middle of a sentence, without the slightest effort, and carry on from there, as soon as the story-teller 'on duty' took a bite of his bread, or blew his nose with his bare hand, afterwards carefully stroking his dark, wavy moustache. It was, incidentally, not only the handsome moustache, cared for so lovingly by each, which made the brothers seem like twins; but, in addition, they were of similar build, nor did one of them move a single step without the other. They ate together, they went together to the latrine, and they emerged from the barracks hand-in-hand, as it were, when the camp bell rang for parade. In brief, they were most perfectly and touchingly attached to one another, and the real reason for this attachment was the prophecy.

For this prophecy in which they firmly believed separated them off from the common misery, and enfolded them like a protective cloud, as it were, rendering them invisible and invulnerable to the fate which slunk greedily around among the rest. They were no longer poor mortals, hiding away in torment from the riddle of a doubtful future, but like gods they saw what was to come to them; even more, they saw that good was to come to them. And it was this knowledge which gave them the placid friendliness of penguins and enabled them to endure with equanimity the life which, even by then, seemed to the others to be almost intolerable.

This is how the prophecy came to be made.

* * *

Fritz Becklam, the elder of the two brothers, a peasant's son from Schleswig Holstein, received an order, as a corporal, in the winter of 1943-4, to establish a strongpoint in a village of Central Russia in order to fight the partisans. The name of the village, if Becklam's story was to be believed, was Penniszevitschi or the like, but this is not material to the story. Becklam had entered this village with a squad of volunteers—that is, Russian soldiers who after being taken prisoner were fighting voluntarily on the German side against their own countrymen—and made his billet in a simple but clean peasant's house (he always emphasized the 'clean' when telling the story). The woman of the house, the widow of a driver who had been killed at the very beginning of the war, gave up her own room to the corporal and lived with her eight-year-old son in the kitchen. Although Maria, as Becklam called her in his story, was bound to fear the punishment and the revenge of the partisans who were living in the woods all around the village, and of course had their spies in the village as well, she nevertheless served the foreign soldier in the most friendly way. Night and day she surrounded the handsome and cheerful man with a motherly and self-forgetful affection. Soon, in fact, she avowed to him that she even prayed for him when he went out on his dangerous duties. Very soon, however, he succeeded in welding his rather savage band of Russians into such a useful unit that the partisans in the neighbourhood preferred to lie quietly, and, as he put it, they 'spat round his villages in a wide circle'.

Soon after taking up his quarters in Maria's house, Becklam noticed that, especially late at night, strangers, mostly women, sat in his landlady's kitchen and addressed her in urgent, subdued tones, until the deep friendly voice of his hostess, flowing in a quiet, conspiratorial stream, silenced the unrest of the questioners. Late one evening, made ill-at-ease by this mysterious traffic, the corporal unexpectedly entered the kitchen, and saw several strangers, men and women, picturesquely grouped round the table, while his kind landlady was seated at it, strangely erect and rigid. There was a light on her face as she listened and gazed into the distance, which gradually changed into a dark and solemn expression of strength and suffering. She had a pack of cards lying before her on the table, and she pointed now to one and now to another of the exposed figures. She had still not said a word, but the words seemed to be rising up in her, spilling from her lips at first in a broken murmur, and then with increasing strength and decision while her countenance relaxed and grew bright.

'Card-reading', thought the German. He had come across it often enough in Russia. He was really just a little disappointed that even this nice, sensible woman should give herself to this trash. The next day, when she brought him his breakfast, he teased her about her superstition. She replied quietly that he should not make fun of it, but rather allow her to tell his future from the cards. The corporal would not hear of it. He dropped his chaffing tone and took her seriously to task:

such nonsense, he said, was possible only in Russia, where the people were entangled in every kind of frenzy, in spite of their indefatigable propaganda to establish the Russian people as the most enlightened and progressive in the world. But she had better keep away from him with that sort of thing, he had no time for that kind of hocus-pocus; and what were all these people after in the kitchen every day? He would not put up with it any longer; it was well known how many spies and agents of the partisans were still about in the villages; he had no desire to waken some morning with a knife in his throat. In any case it was a stinking job for him, an honest and decent soldier, to have to play cowboys and Red Indians here, instead of leading a section of proper German infantrymen, as befitted a corporal.

Maria wept. But she made no reply, nor did she cease to serve the corporal loyally. On the succeeding evenings he heard, with his command of the language, several conversations in the kitchen and at the door of the house, which clearly showed that Maria energetically dismissed her visitors, in spite of their importunate pleas. This obedience pleased the German, and in order to make a friendly return, he no longer refused when she begged him, almost implored him, once again, to have the cards laid for him, 'at least for the following day'. If the cards should deceive, then she would never again trouble him with her prophecies.

So the same evening they sat down together at the kitchen table in the candlelight. Once again the corporal noticed with a slight shiver how the broad soft face of the Russian woman became rigid and hard, as though a mask were laid over it. A terrible, sinister and solemn strength spread across her features, and while her finger fell now on this, now on that card, as though drawn by a string, the words struggled from her breast as though she was in labour, coming first in separate shreds, in a halting whisper, then more resolute and clear and finally sharp and authoritative. She told the corporal that he would receive seven things in the post the next day, ' three large and four small '.

This was simply incredible to the German, even ridiculous, since he rarely received more than two letters or postcards at one time; and besides, he had no intention of fetching the mail the next day from his base.

The next morning he had a visit from the battalion quartermaster-sergeant, with whom he was on friendly terms. And while the two men sat and chatted in Becklam's room the visitor said casually, ' There's a lot of post, Fritz. Just a moment.' He went back to his truck and brought a parcel and two smaller packets, three letters and a postcard.

That was a bit thick! thought Corporal Becklam. How on earth could Maria know of these seven missives? When later in his astonishment and amusement he asked her about them, she smiled in a friendly way and quietly said that she had already consulted the cards again and was ready to foretell the events of the coming days to him in the same way.

He was very interested! the corporal found himself saying.

14

And Maria, with a characteristic gesture, put her finger quickly to the tip of her nose and announced in a serious voice that the next day there would appear at the corporal's the messenger of a man . . . of a man— she could not say exactly who it was . . . someone who was half private and half official . . . at any rate this man would invite the corporal, along with his landlady, to his house, and the corporal would see fit to accept the invitation. On the journey to this man's house the corporal would have a trifling accident from which no serious consequences were to be feared.

'We shall see,' said Becklam, in whose eyes the woman's certainty and clear-cut predictions began to seem somewhat ominous.

Early the next morning a young fellow came to the corporal with a message from the priest of the nearby larger village. This priest had been re-established in his office by the Germans, and since he had influence over the people it was better to have him as friend than foe. Becklam therefore accepted the invitation with thanks and sent his greetings. The messenger bowed, turned, and prepared to take his leave. But at the door he turned again and said he had forgotten to ask the corporal in his master's name if he had any objection to Maria Ivanovna, his landlady, coming too. She was well known to the priest, and since she knew the way to his house, he wished to invite her at the same time to celebrate his birthday (or name-day, Becklam had forgotten which) with him.

It was a cold, clear winter's day. As the corporal, on the way to the priest's, was driving his two frisky horses

along a slight curve before a wooden bridge over a
stream, the sledge for no obvious reason began to skid,
and the man, taken by surprise, was hurled against the
railing of the bridge. For a moment he felt a slight
pain in his chest; but he was able to drive on, and at
the priest's birthday party, in spite of the shaking he
had received, he was a cheerful guest. The next day
the pains were bad enough to compel him to take to his
bed for several days. Then he was able to get up and
perform his duties as before.

That was the beginning.

For now Corporal Becklam had half begun to believe
in the cards, or rather in the woman's inexplicable gift
of clairvoyance. Since a belief of this sinister kind is
never nourished from itself, but in contrast with genuine
belief always hungers for fresh proofs, Maria did not
have to ask her lodger twice to have the cards prophesy
to him again. He himself wanted it, in fact he wanted
it so impatiently that Maria, who still believed in God,
in a sudden access of fear warned him that in all this
he must always give God alone the honour; for only in
alliance with God would everything that she had to
prophesy reach a good end. The corporal who accepted,
without thinking, what he had learned by rote, and still
allowed God a place in his scheme of things, readily
acknowledged his belief in order to pacify the Russian.
She still took every opportunity to repeat her warning,
since she was really fond of the man and cared for the
good of his soul.

Then the woman said to him that he should beware
of a big black-haired man who hated him and wished

him evil. The corporal at first thought that this enemy must be one of his subordinates, a savage and dark Russian. But the next day Maria added the information that the enemy was not a Russian but a German, who would sit opposite Becklam at a dinner, and would be envious of an honour paid to him.

Three days later Becklam was ordered to report to his battalion. Shortly before he mounted the sledge, Maria took him aside once more and whispered in his ear that he need not fear his enemy as he would be killed the next day. When the corporal reported to his Commanding Officer, a little uncertain what bad news awaited him, the major greeted him like a personal friend and took him at once into a room where many officers and warrant officers of the Field Security Police were gathered for a special celebration. In the presence of them all the major welcomed the astonished corporal, making special reference to his services in fighting the partisans during the past months, thanked him for his brave work and presented him with a decoration. He then invited him to take his seat beside him.

Now everyone present, as is customary on such occasions, raised his glass again and again to drink Becklam's health, and Becklam, who was certainly not insensible to such honours and praise, was very happy. After a while, however, when he raised his head for the first time out of the intoxication of joy and self-esteem in which he was sunk, he saw the 'dark man' against whom Maria had warned him, sitting directly opposite him. He was a sergeant called Mielke, whom the corporal knew very well, who was regarded in the reserve as an ambitious and unscrupulous slave-driver. This Mielke was staring at the guest of honour with ill-concealed envy; he never toasted him, but made it plain several times in the course of the evening that he considered the praise to be too extravagant. When all was said and done, everyone in the regiment just did his duty, and Becklam was by no means the only one who had successes to his credit. And in tones loud enough for everyone to hear, the sergeant described an operation which he had planned for the following day which with one blow would put out of action every partisan in his area.

This occurred at the moment when everyone had already left their seats and were standing about in little groups, animated and heated by the strong drinks, equally ready for fun and for argument. Becklam went up to the sergeant and urged him to think again about what he was proposing to do. His plan would certainly miscarry. It was a matter of course that the sergeant should take offence and shout out that this was really the limit; some people's success went to their heads so badly that they thought they could control other people's lives as well.

'Whether you listen or not, Mielke,' Becklam persisted, 'I know what I know. And I tell you, don't go out on this job to-morrow. You won't come back.'

'What d'you mean by that?' 'Go easy old fellow.' 'How do you know what is to happen?' came suddenly from every side. And since the corporal did not want to go into details, the others, too, became a little suspicious of him and did not know what to think of the whole matter, so that their feelings swung round to the sergeant's side as solidly as he could desire.

But the next day he did not return from his operation against the partisans. After a long search they found him dead in the forest, fearfully mutilated, along with his whole squad. The corporal received the news as a matter of course; he had already gone so far. When shortly afterwards he went on leave, he reported to his Commanding Officer; then he went to the clerk's room and said to his friend the quartermaster-sergeant: 'It's a pity: I shall not see him again.'

When he returned from leave, the Commanding Officer was dead. His car had been shot up by partisans. Maria had foretold it.

Chapter Two

FRITZ BECKLAM hated Russia, the bare hopelessness of its plains, its endless marshy forests, behind every tree of which murder, torment, uncertainty and peril lay in wait for him. How often he had cursed the day which had brought him to Russia, especially to this miserable region of partisans, where 'the devil sought his own'. And yet this time something drew him back, he himself did not know what. When Maria met him with joyful glance, and once more surrounded him with her obedient, motherly love, then the young man felt at home. But almost immediately he asked her what was to happen now.

Maria indicated that they had to part, though only for a short time. He would come to a house which was standing on its head. He would shoot from this house, and the house would be his salvation. He would stay in a village, and there a young and pretty girl would love him. He would follow the girl over a cemetery wall and everything would be lovely and gay.

But after that—her face grew dark—there would be an accident, and he would have gloomy days. First he would be wounded while in his Commanding Officer's car, both in the shoulder and the temple; but he need have no fear—not yet. After that she saw him in a house in the earth. There was great danger there. He must leave this house as quickly as possible and go into the house next to it, and in this way he would be saved. Then he would stand beside a bog and keep guard. Two Russians would come with the morning light, and he would take them prisoner. But after that would come a third man, who would not let himself be taken. And here again was danger. Danger, trouble and sorrow. But he must not fear. Not yet.

This was indeed more than a prophecy for the next day. Becklam listened to it with many a headshake, and said condescendingly: 'Maria, Maria!' but in reality he believed every word the Russian told him, and impatiently awaited the fulfilment of the prediction.

A few days later the order came for him to set out immediately with his squad, in order that they might take part in a larger operation against partisans in the region of Ossinushka (or the like). As Becklam mounted the sledge which was to take him at the head of his party to Ossinushka, where his battalion lay, Maria whispered in his ear that he would not stay in Ossinushka but would move on from there. How long did he have to stay there, then? Becklam wanted to know. For in his orders he had been warned to prepare for a stay of some weeks, perhaps even months. Maria replied that he would not stay there long. 'Well, how long? Perhaps a week?' 'No, not a single day.' 'Then half a day?' 'No, only two hours.'

There was another queer thing! The corporal

laughed in the woman's face. Then she added that from Ossinushka to their new destination they would have such a frightful journey that the hair on their heads would bristle with horror. Their truck would many times run on two wheels, and everyone would think his last hour had come. But here, too, Fritz, and everyone else with him, need have no fear. For nothing would happen to any of them. Only one man would be slightly injured.

When Becklam reported to his battalion at Ossinushka the staff-sergeant allocated a billet to him and told him to settle down in it. He would get his orders the next day. But Becklam answered that he would not unpack his kit at all, since he would be staying only a few hours. The staff-sergeant, who already knew of Becklam's obsession, smiled and shook his head and let the corporal go his own way. But scarcely had he told the clerks in his office of this new foolery of Becklam's, to which they listened with avidity, than he had to take a personal telephone call, the gist of which was that Becklam and his men were to be sent on to a place called Nikolskoje. A truck had to be put at his disposal immediately, in order that he might reach Nikolskoje that same evening.

Precisely two hours later the truck was ready to leave. As Becklam was packing his men and equipment aboard, he shouted in annoyance: 'I suppose you couldn't find an older wreck?' And indeed the vehicle was not cal- culated to inspire confidence, the driver even less so, sitting dully at the wheel and staring glassy-eyed ahead. Becklam saw that the man was not sober, and it was really his duty to have a word with him or even to find a new driver. But he was now so deeply under the spell of his prophetess that he did neither, but dumbly trusted that all would be well.

Scarcely had they set off than the corporal regretted with all his heart that he had not got rid of the driver, who was either very drunk or mad, or at least that, in order to protect his men, he had not sat beside the moron. For they tore on recklessly, and when Maria had prophesied that the truck would sometimes run not on four but on two wheels, she was literally right. The men were tossed about as though they were in convulsions. Scarcely were they all jammed together on the left side, running for a horrible moment on the two left wheels alone, than a wild jolt hurled them back to the right; in brief, it was more like a journey on an enormous cake-walk than on a truck. The further they hurtled the keener was the corporal's impression that he was at the mercy of a leaping, swaying, circling devil; it was even too much for the phlegmatic Russians, and if Becklam, thanks to his prophecy, had not been almost immune to fear and terror, he would really have thought that his last hour had come.

They reached their destination late at night. As they dismounted only one man complained of pain in the shoulder. Early the next day they were added to the strength of the battalion for a united operation. They set off along a railway embankment over wet and dirty snow, constantly on the alert for strong partisan forces which had been surrounded by German units, and if all went according to plan were to be pressed back against the railway line. This line had hitherto been exposed to constant attack by the partisans. Only the previous day the Russians had succeeded in mining and derailing a train carrying munitions and food. One wagon had been overturned beside the level embankment and lay on the dirty snow with its wheels upwards, a miserable picture of destruction.

At about the level of this overturned and half-destroyed wagon, Becklam met with sudden and violent fire from the wood, which ran along both sides of the line at a distance of about fifty yards. Since the fire came simultaneously from right and left, the only hope of safety lay in the corporal taking refuge, along with most of his men, in the overturned wagon. They had scarcely done this when it occurred to the ambushed man that this must be the 'house on its head' of which Maria had spoken. He immediately became calm and hopeful, in fact he was sorely tempted to joke about the truly comic way in which the prophecy had been fulfilled. The Russian volunteers gazed at him in depression and fear, for they knew that the partisans would not be satisfied with shooting them, should they catch them. But the corporal was now so sure of himself that something of his untroubled resolution was imparted to the Russians. He ordered them to bring the machine-gun into position and to put their 'house on its head' in as strong a state of defence as was possible. And it was not at all bad, for all kinds of heavy planks, full boxes and sacks provided additional protection from the enemy's bullets. Even when, some time later, enemy cavalry to the strength of a squadron broke suddenly out of the woods and tried to storm the remarkably toughly defended German strongpoint, the corporal did not lose his nerve for a moment. He himself lay behind the machine-gun, and fired so accurately at the onrushing horsemen that their attack broke down painfully and bloodily. . . . Soon afterwards more German sections pushed forward along the embankment, and the partisans retreated. Of Becklam's men two were dead, four wounded, and the remaining fourteen uninjured.

Towards evening, without having won a decisive success, the German sections, together with the Russian volunteers, withdrew to the village of Nikolskoje. Becklam received orders to relinquish his Russian squad and to hold himself in readiness for the next day, since he was chosen for a special task. After the sleepless night and the taxing day of fighting he felt quite exhausted and sought without delay for a billet for the night. He was shown to a dirty hovel, where he was to share the one room with the whole family. While he stood in the door, annoyed and uncertain, and almost resolved not to stay, he heard one of the women at the stove say: 'He doesn't like it, you see, Nina. Take him with you, he's a fine fellow.'

In the uncertain light of the lamp on the table, he had only an indistinct view of the person addressed. A white, firm, round face, framed in a kerchief. But he heard her soft laughter, and it encouraged him to approach the stove and to look. Then the first woman went on (in Russian, and probably she thought that the soldier did not understand her): 'Now look! He has seen you now, little one. Don't be stupid, you won't find a finer fellow so late in the evening.'

'Don't you know any other quarters for me?' Becklam addressed the corner brusquely.

She who had been addressed as 'Nina' and 'little one' stood up and went past Becklam to the door. She was perhaps seventeen years old, big and strong; but there was still something of the child in the movement with which she now turned back to the man and nodded to him: 'Come.'

The corporal took his pack again and followed her, first along the street with its wet and dirty soft snow, then up a short side street. . . . They stood before a half broken-down gate, and the girl turned again to the German soldier with the same lovely, reserved, maidenly gesture, slightly bowed her round white face, and said with a smile: 'Across the churchyard. It's nearer and not so dirty.'

'Of course, the churchyard!' thought Becklam. The girl, 'pretty and young'. And where is the wall? There it was: a low, half-ruined little wall; and Nina had already, with an energetic movement, kirtled up her skirt, in order to climb over the wall at a point which had been flattened by many passers-by. From the other side she turned to the German expectantly, and even naïvely stretched out a friendly hand to help him. . . .

When Becklam later spoke of this girl he always emphasized that he had of course 'done nothing' to her. She was still innocent, and it was not his way 'to seduce children'. All the same he had fallen head over heels in love with the pretty Nina, at first sight; he didn't deny it. After she had helped him down from the wall into the pitch darkness, she kept her hand in his, just as

26

if he were her father or her brother; and so she led him to her parents' home, a clean little new house beside the electrically driven mill of which her father was the manager. The broad and strapping Russian, who had a smattering of German, evidently thought it better to be friendly to the foreign soldier and to offer him the best room and food, than to make things unpleasant for himself with a discontented guest. So he at once had his living-room made ready for him for the night, and noisily urged on his wife and daughter to bring ' the officer' food and drink, which was speedily forthcoming in great quantity. Nor did he fail to curse the wicked partisans who had nothing better to do than to disturb the peace and rob decent folk. And if the corporal had reason to doubt the honesty of these theatrical declarations, still he decided not to enquire closely into the matter, but to make the best of the situation and to enjoy himself as though everything were as it appeared.

As far as Nina was concerned, the corporal was inclined to think that she was not pretending, but had a real liking for him. This view was natural to his masculine vanity, the feeling that he was irresistible to women, which was not surprising in this handsome, peasant Don Juan. But even Nina's parents seemed to find nothing strange in the fact that their daughter sat so close to the German, held his hand, and later laid her head on his shoulder. For Becklam himself the whole situation, after the heavy day, was immensely satisfying. He felt genuine affection not only for the girl but also for her parents. So after the meal he took out his wallet and showed them the pictures of his mother, his brothers, and his village, one by one, and was delighted with the child-like wonder and warm interest of his hosts. In all this he showed the best side of his character: he paid compliments not only to the daughter but also to the mother, for Nina's mother was still young and a picture of glowing health. He smiled at the girl with his best smile, smoothing her fine fair ringlets off her brow. Now and then he uttered a most realistic yelp like a little dog, and performed other jokes which delighted the simple hearts of the women. And he felt with increasing happiness that he pleased the young creature by his side, that she nestled ever more warmly against him and repeated his name more and more frequently: 'Fritz, Fritz.'

And deep in his heart he thought approvingly: 'That Maria! What a first-rate evening she has arranged for me! How nice of her to prophesy this young blood for me!' No, he certainly did not want to harm her, the pretty little one. But to flirt a little late at night, to play the gallant and to sense her warm presence, to sun himself a little in the feeling of his irresistibility, that did him good. After all, he was too tired for anything else. . . . When he stole a kiss from her she did not take it amiss. He kissed her in her parents' presence, and all four laughed happily at his tenderness. Certainly no strict etiquette reigned here, nor would the mother, very likely, have protested against similar treatment. And then, of course, Nina . . . Nina . . . he really liked her, there was no denying it. But Nina's parents were decent folk. When at last they said good night, for it was late, Nina remained seated, perfectly

28

naturally, nor did her parents ask her to accompany them.

'Are you tired, little Nina?' asked Becklam, after they had sat quietly for quite a while nestled together. For after her parents had gone, Nina had not said a word but only stroked the man's hand as though in complete self-forgetfulness. He himself, now that he was no longer laughing and talking, was suddenly overcome by great tiredness. His limbs were leaden, he could scarcely keep his eyes open.

'Tired?' he repeated.

The girl shook her head slowly, without embarrassment. 'But I am, Nina,' he said. 'I can't hold my head up any more.'

She laughed silently and pressed him tenderly down on to the sofa. The corporal made no resistance. 'What strength these Russian women have!' he thought, as Nina took hold of him under the armpits and pulled him to the high end of the sofa. Then she raised his feet as well. Now he was perfectly comfortable, he lacked nothing.

'Take your kerchief off, Nina,' he said sleepily.

She obeyed. As she laid the kerchief in her lap and bent her head, her luxuriant hair streamed forward and fell like a soft golden flame over her temples and cheeks. Nina pushed it negligently back. And as she raised her arms the man looked at her and thought: 'Heavens, she is no longer a child. Not she! She has everything a woman should have. And twice over!'

And then, while his senses swayed into sleep, he was overcome by a powerful sensation of which he was later to give only a dull and confused account. It was as though a great power had suddenly streamed from the girl. He had never experienced the like before, not even with Maria. At school he had learned about the enchantress, the Lorelei, who had suddenly so bewitched a sailor on the Rhine by her song that from sheer infatuation and enchantment he did not know what he was doing. Nina did not sing, she was simply there, and raised her strong arms and pushed back her hair.

And yet it seemed to him that she offered him her whole body; so plainly and defencelessly, foolishly and imprudently, as seductively as . . . as . . . the devil alone knew what! But Nina was no witch, she was not cunning. But all at once there was this magic power, which drew him on and made his senses reel and his tongue cleave to the roof of his mouth with—with what, in fact? With fear—was that possible? You can laugh, but I was in fact almost afraid of the stupid Russian creature beside me, afraid of the child with the great warm woman's body! It was a good thing, Becklam was accustomed to add at this point, that he was so terribly tired, otherwise something would have happened, my dear fellows. For it seemed as though all the women of the world, the soft and the savage, the ugly and the beautiful, were tearing at him, tearing at his heart so that he was in pain. . . .

But apparently all that happened was that he drew Nina down to him in his last waking moment, and she let him do it; and then he fell asleep. How long this sleep might have lasted he did not know; but after some time he wakened with the feeling that something had roused him. The lamp was out. In the faint moonlight he saw above him the round, pale face of the girl, watchful, smiling lovingly upon him.

'What is it?' he said in German. His instinct told him with utter certainty that danger threatened. 'What is it?' he repeated in Russian. 'Did you hear something?'

'A shot,' replied the girl, peacefully stroking his hair.

'I must get up,' said the man, and straight away he was fully awake. He had slept deep and sound, and was refreshed. He sat up, tried to sit up. . . . But the girl shook her head, with a tranquil and stubborn smile, and pressed him on the shoulders so firmly that he sank down again, astonished and almost amused.

'What is going on here?' he wondered. 'Is she really a witch? Or what is she?' He was quite clear that he must get up at once. He was an old and experienced soldier and he smelt danger in the air; he sensed it in every limb. But this shining round face, of which all he could clearly perceive was the whites of her eyes and her teeth, deprived him of his will. The warm hands on his shoulders, whose grasp was now soft and kind once more. . . . He pulled the girl's head roughly down to him; he felt the sudden need to prove to her that he was her master. He kissed her large, friendly mouth, the warm lips which were yielded so willingly, and surely were never kissed before, and yet seemed to know so much of love. But his disquietude and a feeling of oppression and evil enchantment were not dissipated, not even when Nina began to stroke him more vigorously and pressed her firm breast against him.

31

'Heavens, that *is* shooting!' ejaculated the corporal, seriously troubled, and annoyed with the girl.

But Nina only shook her head again obstinately. Her heavy soft hair flowed over the man's face, it had a strong, sharp scent, like fresh-cut hay on a summer night. The girl herself now seemed to fall more and more under the spell of a powerful enchantment. Her smile grew rigid, her eyes dilated as in ecstasy, and she clutched the man's uniform tensely. A power which rose out of the abyss of her sex seemed to move through her body, to make it tense, to bend it and to render it insensate by its demand for surrender. Every attempt which he made to rise from her helpless and sensual embrace was met by a stronger and almost furious pressure. As he said later, he had never experienced the like, and he was no novice where women were concerned. For she was no loose woman, nor was she sophisticated or full of tricks. But she was in an ecstasy, she was on fire, everything stirred in her at once; and finally there burst from her breast a wild moaning, which broke as it were in deep waves of grief over the poor corporal.

And now there was not only shooting to be heard, but voices as well and a wild, drunken roar. Nearer and nearer. With a tremendous effort Becklam freed himself from the girl. He had to push her away, to lift her off, there was no other way.

He ran to the door, and looked out cautiously. . . . Rifle fire. Then for the first time a machine-gun. Quite near. As though they were shooting straight at the house. The corporal looked round. Where were his things? Yes, they were still there. He looked back at the sofa. Nina sat bolt upright. Like a sleep-walker she slowly rose and approached the man. He signed to her to sit down again. Then he took up his pack, jammed his forage-cap on his head, and went out.

There was that accursed moon, three-quarters full. The corporal waited until a dirty cloud had drifted over its silly cheese-face. Now! He saw the wall of the churchyard, perhaps thirty steps away. . . . Fine. It had turned beautifully dark; but if only the damned shooting would stop for a moment! Obviously the pickets were withdrawing into the village from the out-skirts until they reached reinforcements. He would have to get over the wall and join the others as quickly as pos-sible. It was careless of him to seek out such a billet apart from the rest. Fine! The machine-gun had at last ceased firing. . . . He leapt forward, across the yard, up to the wall, swung himself over, and ducked down. . . . As he did this he cast one last glance back at the house he had just left, and saw Nina emerging quietly and following him, as though she were drawn by a string, still moving like a sleep-walker. But she had taken only a single step away from the house when he saw her quietly sink down on to her face. . . . Good God, she'd had it! The machine-gun had begun again. Oh, accursed Russia! There she lay. The dream was over. Over.

And while the corporal stumbled hastily forward, picking his way between overgrown graves, still half hidden beneath patches of dirty snow, and ghostly, lean-ing, double crosses, he felt all at once an immense pity for the young creature who had sunk down so silently and almost ceremonially, like a poor sacrificial victim. And in truth he was guilty of her death, in literal truth. Although of course he could do nothing about it when she ran out after him. She knew that there was shooting outside. He had told her to keep sitting. He had liked her. Dear heavens, he had really done her no harm. . . . But now, there it was. He could have howled with grief, so deep did it go in him. Oh, this accursed war! This thrice-accursed, festering war!

And all the time, as he ran on through the slippery, dirty spring snow, the corporal saw the lovely, infatuated girl sinking on her face so horribly, like a doll which has fallen down in the shop window. God knows, he thought again, I could really have loved that girl.

He encountered German soldiers who were going up each side of the village street under the command of a lieutenant. He reported to the officer and was given command of a section of the men. Then suddenly it entered his head—'Maria foresaw it. She did not say it clearly, but she spoke of the girl, and of something sad that would happen.' And he thought also: 'Everything is determined, anyway. It had to be, and that's that. I am not guilty. I did her no harm. How could I help it when she began to blaze up like that? No, I shall ask Maria if she foresaw it. Surely she foresaw it. And it simply had to be. . . . Always the same circling thoughts. It's enough to drive a man crazy!'

Then all at once he was seized with a terrible fury against Maria. Suddenly he hated her prophecies, under whose spell he had fallen so dreadfully. He almost

34

blamed her for Nina's death. She had not only foreseen it, but she had also brought it about, the witch!
She had grudged her, the young girl, her little bit of
life! But there was no use thinking about it. He
would only lose his head. Let things happen as they
must. And if his own hour had not yet come, when
he, too, had to bite the dust, then good—in fact, all the
better. . . .

While they were still busy driving the partisans out
of the village, Becklam was summoned to his new
Commanding Officer who was leading the action in
person. 'Becklam,' the colonel said, 'a signal has
just come in that our munitions and rations convoy
has been attacked in the woods three miles from
Nikolskoje, and is at a standstill. Take my scout car,
two armoured vehicles and a mortar section. See to it
that you get the convoy moving again. We need it.'

Chapter Three

As the corporal, at the head of his little armoured column, approached the dark wall of the wood, he could hear the furious rattle of machine-gun fire rising and falling, interspersed by individual clear bursts of rifle-fire, ending abruptly, foolishly. He gave the order to speed up the advance, and for the mortar team to be at the ready.

They had scarcely penetrated two miles into the wood when he saw, in the twilight of the ugly winter morning, the heap of ambushed trucks some distance ahead of them on the road. The ambush had obviously come only from one side of the road, for the enemy fire was coming from the right. Without further ado the corporal signalled his mortar team to fire several rounds rapidly into the wood. . . . The enemy fire weakened, but did not cease. Becklam edged nearer to the abandoned trucks, and fired again. Through the narrow slit in his armoured car he watched splintering and splitting trees. Again the firing weakened. The partisans must have realized that things were not going well for them. Behind them Becklam heard the dull firing of the mortar. That was the men from the armoured truck, who were carrying out their orders first to cover the wood with fire before moving in to the attack.

'And that will come at any moment now,' thought the corporal grimly.

At that moment he was struck on the shoulder and temple. He put his hand up to his head and his fingers were covered with blood. The man beside him uttered a curse, pulled out his first-aid pack and said: 'That might have been your eye. An explosive bullet. Right through the observation slit, grazed on the edge, and exploded. A nice job!'

Becklam remained calm. He had known of this wound. He was not interested; it was not worth talking about. But one thing was perfectly clear: everything was predetermined and happened as it had to happen. Even as he thought this, there rose again before his eyes, in the thick of the battle, the picture of how Nina . . . No, he was not to blame for that. What had he done with the girl? He had teased her a little, stroked her and loved her a little, and that was all. That was what he was a young man for, and a soldier, who might bite the dust any day. That was what war was for, and life, too. But he was not to blame, and that was that. Once for all.

In the days which followed Corporal Becklam forgot to brood. Day and night he was in action; and whenever there was a lull his senses immediately left him and he fell asleep, lying, sitting, or standing. On the fourth day the Germans succeeded in striking the partisans so hard that they were driven, after heavy losses, deep into the woods. Towards the evening of this day the corporal was ordered to occupy a forward position with his new section of German infantry, in order to prevent any fresh infiltration by the partisans. He found an old trench-line with some dug-outs, probably Russian defences at the beginning of the war. As the line was well protected by broad marshy land, Becklam decided to establish himself and his men in it.

He put out sentries, but not many. For he did not believe that the greatly reduced enemy would risk a fresh attack that night. He thought at first of disposing the remainder of his men equally among the three wooden dug-outs; but it turned out that the central one was not only the largest, but by far the warmest and best preserved. So the corporal yielded to his men's pleas and arranged for the whole section to put up there. But he had scarcely brought them all into the central dug-out—an operation which was, of course, accompanied by a certain amount of noise—when Maria's prophecy flashed across his mind, that he would take possession of a house in the earth, but would—fortunately for him—evacuate it again and move into the neighbouring house. His immediate instinct was to accept the prophecy wholeheartedly. Had not everything which the woman had prophesied with her accursed witchcraft come true to the last iota, the little good as well as the great deal of evil? Was there any point at all in rebelling with human power against this obscurely ordained fate? Did he bring about this fate, or did another? Was he guilty of everything as it came and had to come? Was he to take it upon his conscience that his men found death in the very place where they thought themselves most secure?

The corporal issued the order that the central dug-out should be evacuated immediately. The men cursed and thought their corporal had taken leave of his senses; but they obeyed, wakened one another and even made an effort to be as noiseless as possible in leaving the shelter and dividing themselves amongst the two others, which were thirty to forty yards away on each side. They had not been settled for half an hour in their new quarters, which were certainly not to be compared with the first, since they had suffered from artillery fire and offered little protection from the penetrating cold—they had scarcely ceased expressing their disapproval by muttered grumbles and curses, when suddenly such a furious noise of battle arose outside that even those who had fallen asleep started up in bewilderment. In a trice Becklam was outside, and cautiously raising his head he saw that the central dug-out was being violently attacked. Hand grenades were pelting on the window-slits and on the entrance to the little wooden stronghold: two machine-guns barked incessantly, and now he saw that dark figures were advancing, one leap at a time and all together, towards the heavily bombarded shelter, in order to take it by storm.

In less than a minute the corporal had a machine-gun brought into position; and at the very moment when the partisans closed in from every side on the central dug-out, which from their observation the previous evening they clearly thought was the only occupied one, he opened fire upon them and ordered his men to throw their grenades.

39

The next morning the Germans found four bodies round the shelter. The trails of blood leading away from it told them that the Russian losses were even greater; they had taken their wounded with them. Becklam noted this new military success without great joy, but rather with a kind of grim, ironical, malicious satisfaction in face of the unknown Author of all the things which were here being played out in accordance with such uncannily exact rules.

In the grey of the dawn, when he himself relieved one of the exhausted sentries in the trench, he did it in a kind of vague and weary curiosity. He wanted to see . . . No, he really did not want to see anything more; he had had enough. If only he could sleep again, have a proper long night's sleep! His wet feet were beginning to freeze; from the first winter of the war he had old frost-bites on his feet, which tormented him again and again. What a life! . . . And now he really did see two figures creeping through the marsh, with heads cautiously ducked like beasts of the forest. They drew near like shadows, in the first grey light, but the stupid creatures were making almost exactly for the point where the corporal was standing. He let them come nearer, very near. Only when they were ten paces away did he raise himself slightly out of the trench, point his automatic pistol at them and cry out: '*Stoij!* Halt! '

The two Russians raised their arms wildly, and surrendered at once. When he ordered them to come nearer he could read on their faces, despite the dull half-light, both fear and shock. They were two elderly men in ragged, padded clothes and fur caps; they had no weapons, but of course they could have dropped them into the marsh to right and left of the narrow foot-track. They were clever at that. They declared that they had been pressed into service by the partisans and that they had just succeeded in escaping and now wanted to get back to their village. Becklam handed them both over to his men. He had had too much trouble already from just such harmless-seeming men; his superiors could decide what was to happen to them. It was not his business. Now he awaited the third man and then he could call it a day. Things went their course. There was nothing to be done about it.

He had to wait a full half-hour before the 'third man' emerged. He came differently from the other two, more swiftly and nimbly, in short leaps, turning his head and body this way and that, not unlike a deer that stops, and sniffs, and spies out the land, then briefly and delicately hastens on, in every movement alert and like a sleep-walker, fine and clear. It was not easy to keep to the right path in the marshes, and at the same time to escape the eyes of the watcher.

Again the same game. There was no difference: the path through the marsh led right up to Corporal Becklam, and when the man was ten paces away in the grey light the German uttered, as before, his curt word of command to halt, at the same time bringing his automatic threateningly to the ready. But this time the man who was addressed did not throw up his hands in shock and numb fear, but though he leapt into the air like a frightened animal, he turned and raced back along the

41

path into the misty twilight of the morning. The corporal's first volley missed him. He sank down, suddenly turned round, kneeling behind a thin bush, and tried to bring his automatic pistol into position. But, before he could fire, the German's second volley had caught him. He cried out softly, rose up again to his full height, and ran. . . . But he ran only a few steps, then stumbled once, and again, as though his too speedy foot had struck on a root. Then he sank down on his knees again, and finally fell heavily forward. . . . He lay there as though felled by an axe.

He was still living when the corporal turned him over. But he was suffering, clearly suffering great agonies in his death struggle. 'Such kids they make into partisans!' said the men, when they had carried him into their shelter. For there was no doubt that this time they had to do with a genuine partisan. The lad carried a Russian automatic pistol and had hand grenades in his pocket. He would not have hesitated to kill every German in cold blood, for he had been taught to do this, or to torture and torment if he had received the order. But all the same . . . 'Oh, God!' thought Becklam, when he saw this child's mouth, out of which welled bloody saliva, and the breaking, beseeching look. 'Oh, God, this accursed war! Why had he to end in this wretched way, instead of rejoicing in his life? Such a silly lad who only wanted to defend his home and who had been told that his fatherland and his State and his Communism were worth a life! What did the poor cur know about politics, about that accursed clique up above who made the war and needed him, and were possessed of the devil!' And suddenly, with hot terror, the corporal thought: 'I have killed him! I have killed him!'

They made a bed for him, as best they could, on a couple of great-coats. The men in the shelter gazed at the dying youngster with an inarticulate mixture of pity and unease. They were accustomed to the sight of dying men: they knew that there was nothing more to be done. A man intent on dying had to be left in peace; and this one was dying normally, simply, without melodrama, he was a strong young Russian of the forest. . . . But all the same! The corporal could not take his eyes off the torn child's face, across which a waxen paleness spread rapidly. The narrow eyes were fixed on him so beseechingly, without hate, in the helpless innocence of an animal near its end. For the second time the corporal wiped away the foam from his mouth, stroked his thick hair from his brow, opened his greasy padded jacket, laid another coat under his head. Now at last, at last he was dead, with one long, low moan. Finished. I have killed him. I, Corporal Fritz Becklam, I have killed him like a deer in the forest. Not with a bull's eye, he had to be tortured for a while, but all the same—he is dead. Better than the other way round. Better than if he had got me. Anyway, it had to be. Maria foretold it. Accursed fate determined it. I cannot change it.

But if he had only been able to forget that poor child's face, that nice open boy's face. He could not forget it, days and weeks later he saw that look turned up to him in such helpless trust, though it was he who had sent him to agony and to death. Things are certainly not in order! thought the corporal. Something is not right. Who can talk me into believing that I was innocent? I did murder him. I and none other. And even if I had to do it ten times, for otherwise I myself should have had it, it still clings to me, just as the other thing with the girl.

Then he hastily sought shelter from such forebodings and vague surmises in his shabby new wisdom: 'Everything comes as it must,' and 'Accursed war!' And there the matter rested.

When after all this he returned to Maria, the woman started back horrified at his appearance. He recounted the events bitterly; he also let it be seen that he considered her to be a witch, in evil alliance with fate itself. He had an ugly desire to torture both her and himself; but the woman, however much she noted and suffered from the change which had come over him, remained in loyal and friendly patience by his side. Only when he asked for fresh predictions she hesitated for a long time. She said to him, as she had said when they first met: 'Without God it is a sin to know the future.' Or: 'God has everything in His hands.' Or: 'God can change everything if He wills.'

But to all this talk the corporal now turned a deaf ear. In quiet hours he did still think: 'Would that I had never been drawn into all this! I was happier before than I am now. Forgive me my sin, dear God!' But at the same time he had become avid for new prophecies, whether good or evil. He wanted to know, to know! A funny thing, that this woman was suddenly unwilling

44

to come out with it all, and earlier she had so pestered him with her accursed knowledge. She still sat often enough over her devil's cards; but she looked always as though she were gazing into an open grave. And when he at last brought her to speak—it happened shortly before his final departure from her—she burst into tears, a perfect flood of tears. She wept wildly, in great sobs, in a veritable torment of the heart, with her head pressed on the table and her arms hanging down helplessly, heavily.

And when the horrified corporal, who realized for the first time what he had done, had at last brought her back to her senses, she looked at him with terrible seriousness, and said: 'Fritz, there will be a great misfortune, a very great misfortune.'

And she repeated these words many times, always in the same tone, always with the same prophetic seriousness, all the time gazing fixedly at the German.

But when he urged and importuned her to tell him what this great misfortune was which she saw approaching, she only shook her head and repeated in her deep voice: 'There will be a misfortune, Fritz, a great misfortune!' Later she added that there would be 'a great fall'.

The perplexed corporal could make neither rhyme nor reason out of all this. He therefore asked direct: 'Am I to die? Soon?'

Then she let her head fall on the table again and said, dully and despairingly: 'Yes, Fritz, you will die.'

And she wept as before, in wild, terrible, uncontrolled

grief, such as the corporal had never seen in any person before. He was at his wits' end to know what to do. He went out and left her alone.

In the middle of the night the woman roused him from sleep. She shook him so violently that he thought some danger was threatening him. But when he was about to rise and dress quickly, he saw Maria's face; and as during the day it had been ridden by terrible fear and anguish, so now it was illuminated by an equally inexpressible joy. 'Fritz!' she cried, her voice breaking and sobbing for joy, 'Fritz, you will not die! You will *not* die! You will be like a dead man, but you will not die, you will live. The war will be over and your people will have a great fall. You will be a prisoner and you will endure hunger and thirst and illness. But you will not die. You will become well again and go back to your own country.'

And that same night the woman prophesied as she had never prophesied before. It was as though the visions, once they had found the gates, had taken entire possession of this strong human life and were pouring with all their strength into Maria's enthusiastic and wildly disturbed soul. She spoke like a drunken creature, on and on: it was like a birth which could not end, pain and pleasure together. . . . And the man lay there as though under a spell, and listened.

That night Maria told Corporal Becklam that as a prisoner of war he would come into a camp that was neither quite in Poland nor quite in Russia. And there he would meet a brother, one of his brothers—'the one with the moustache'. He would live and work along

46

with him. They would be allocated to the same party, which would be No. 54.

'And when would he go home?' asked the corporal.

He would—he would be injured one day. He would hurt his thumb. Something heavy would fall on it, and the nail would turn blue. When the blue had completely grown out of the nail, then the day and the hour had come. It would be about the time of the greatest festival, and spring would not turn to autumn more than twice before this would be fulfilled. So he must never be afraid: not even when he should one day be taken deeper into Russia. He should not even be afraid when he should one night be taken and thrown into a cell, for all that would pass, as truly as God is in heaven. And these would be the other signs: he would work first in stone, then in wood, and lastly in straw. And he would build houses which were neither houses nor tents, but like both houses and tents. And when all this happened the day of his liberation would be near. Not for him alone, but also for his brother and for all others.

Chapter Four

IN NOVEMBER 1945 P.O.W. Corporal Fritz Becklam
had in fact met his brother Albert in a White Russian
camp—'neither quite in Poland nor quite in Russia'—
and this had happened in the following 'silly way', as
he said. Fritz had one day gone over to the adjoining
hut in order to 'buy' a pair of bootlaces. For in that
hut the prisoners ran a proper barter market, with all
sorts of stolen articles and presents from civilians: you
could have silk stockings in exchange for American
tinned food, for the finest coffee you could have a pair
of solid leather shoes. The corporal could not see bootlaces anywhere that day, though he poked around among
all the bags of flour, sugar, millet, the choice textiles
and straps and spoons and pipes and all the gimcracks of
a proper beggars' and thieves' market. But just as he
was about to leave the hut, disappointed in his search,
his glance fell upon a man who was lying on the pallet
close by the door, with his eyes shut and his hands
clasped behind his head. Like Becklam, the man had a
carefully waved black moustache, whose finely turned
end pointed straight into the heights.

'The devil take us!' thought the corporal. 'It is!'

And Maria's prophecy at once crossed his mind, that he would meet his brother, the one with a moustache, that is, Karl, the eldest, in the camp. He went up to the sleeping man and wakened him. 'Karl, old chap, open your eyes! What d'you think, who's here!'

The man opened his eyes. It was indeed Becklam's brother, not Karl, the eldest, however, but Albert, the youngest, the one Fritz loved most of all, for he had formerly taken him by the hand to school. Albert had grown a moustache while in the prison camp.

Without great difficulty the brothers arranged to sleep next to one another in the same hut, and also to work in the same party outside. When the corporal enquired of the Camp Clerk what the number of their new common working-party was he replied: 'Fifty-four.'

The very number named by Maria.

At that time no more than a hint, a casual mention of these mysterious connections of events, was needed for the whole camp to know the story of the prophecy, as a consequence of which the brothers had discovered one another 'in such a funny way' and had landed together in the working-party which had been foretold. In the joyless, hopeless, homesick atmosphere of the camp, the men concentrated all their wild, sick, distorted hope and longing upon the mysterious prophetic words, which in all the uncertainty of their life seemed to them to be like a firm anchor. In a flash the brothers Becklam became the most sought-after and best-loved people in the camp. They were constantly surrounded by a cluster of poor, ragged prisoners of war, to whom they had to repeat, word for word, the prophecies, fulfilled and still to be fulfilled, of the mysterious Russian woman. In the evenings they were invited to the offices by the cooks, the magazine clerks, and the craftsmen—in other words by the '*élite*' of the camp, that is to say, by those who were in a position to pay for such a joyful message if not with gold at least with a piece of bread or a ladleful of soup. And patiently, or rather proudly and at ease, the two 'penguins' sat evening after evening in one place or another, and sunned themselves in the assurance of their invulnerability, while round about them raged great misery, and death stalked through the camp.

At that time it was dysentery which haunted the camp like a great ghost, weary to death, with hands pressed upon the sick, inflamed body, driven by a tormenting need which could never be satisfied. And whoever was breathed upon by that ghost sank down and in short time was only a shadow or a wretched skeleton that was carried out of the dysentery hut on a stretcher —almost without any contours beneath the dirty cover. One day Corporal Fritz Becklam, too, lay in that hut. He had diarrhœa—it was not bad, just 'the usual'. But the usual quickly became bad. One morning there was blood, and it flowed from him ceaselessly. From hour to hour his sturdy and cheerful strength diminished. It was not long before his blood flowed more feebly through his veins. Black veils fell across his eyes; and the first touch of death's gnarled hand seemed to be upon his heart. At last he was so feeble that he could no longer turn his head; and then he thought: 'Has she not really been wrong this time?' But even thinking was impossible. His whole body was one painful wound, so large and so sore that he lost himself in it. He himself no longer suffered, something greater suffered in him, the creature or the earth, something or other anonymous. That dying young Russian in the wood must also have felt like one single, enormous pain, too great for one individual being. The corporal had always imagined that dying was different, with a peaceful prayer, perhaps, in the arms of someone dear to him, in a clean bed —or on the field of battle. But this? This was no dying, but a pitiful, stupid, snuffing out, a slithering into something alien, hostile, dark. . . .

On the very day on which things were so bad for Fritz Becklam, a Russian medical commission visited the camp and made a great fuss on seeing the high death-rate. And even though everything went on in the old groove soon after the commission's departure, nevertheless the camp medical officers did bestir themselves, when the commission was actually there, to reduce the number of deaths. This proved to be Becklam's salvation. As he could not eat anything, he received substantial injections of glucose, and there occurred the miracle that the man who was considered to be dying turned again out of the shadow of death. Slowly, indeed, but steadily and noticeably, he regained strength and the will to live.

The prophecy had won the victory. The victory over death. From that time it was a crime to doubt Maria's word. Nor did anyone doubt it.

In the winter, when a great convoy was being prepared for Central Russia—at a time when everyone had expected to be repatriated—only a few of the prisoners were frightened by this new reverse. The remarkable thing was that many of the men even queued up to join the convoy, although they knew that it was going to the east. But the brothers Becklam were in it; and with them travelled the guarantee of a good and happy end, even if it went into the depths of hell. For this transport, too, was in the programme. This convoy had been foreseen by Maria, in fact it was, so to speak, a pre-condition of a speedy homecoming. All one had to do was to remain near this prophecy and one had something solid and certain in one's hands. The brothers Becklam, with their complacent and self-assured tranquillity, had become the two camp medicine-men. It is true that they did not contrive good weather, but they contrived a good destiny. So it came about that there was an almost cheerful atmosphere among the men who rolled eastwards in the heavily wired and sealed cattle-trucks.

The first work allocated to the brothers Becklam when they reached the new camp was the building of a road. For some weeks they were separated from the bulk of their fellow-prisoners; they were housed with thirty others in a little hut in the heart of the country, in a bare and god-forsaken district; and since their stories could not rejoice anyone who could show his gratitude in any tangible form, a very hard life began for the pair. From early to late they had to wield great hammers in order to break up the big stones needed for the building of the road: hard labour suitable ' for someone who had murdered his father and mother ', as the men said among themselves. They received only the normal camp rations for this work, and not even all of these, as a part of them was sold by the German cook in league with the Russian guard. In addition, the hot Russian summer was upon them, and that year it spread a perfectly murderous drought across great areas of the Soviet Union.

It was inevitable that the thirty men—with the exception of the cook—very soon became unfit for work. They were returned to the camp and put into the convalescents' hut. Nevertheless, the brothers Becklam had 'worked in stone' as Maria's programme had foreseen. One of the stones had even fallen on Fritz's thumb, which looked like a ripe plum. Now the day of the homeward journey had become calculably near. This was immediately evident to the old friends of the Becklams as well as to many of the new. When after some weeks 'the blue' slowly began to grow out of it, half the camp gazed as though enchanted upon his thumb nail, which guaranteed the happy return of all the prisoners in that very year. And when, about that time, great quantities of straw were brought into the camp to be used for the storing of potatoes and the filling of palliasses, the initiated came running to the Becklams to tell them about this latest confirmation of the prophecy. They laughed and behaved as though the whole thing were just a great joke; but secretly they were on tenterhooks about the succession of signs. They could not conceal their disappointment when Fritz Becklam looked at the little pile of straw behind the cookhouse and shook his head, explaining: 'That's not the right straw.'

The next day the corporal was summoned before the NKVD camp officer, interrogated, then straight away

53

shut up in the camp prison, to which the Russians had given the amusing and harmless name of the 'cooler'. Since Albert had been sent off on the day before this with fifty other prisoners to work at the harvest on a collective farm, the brothers did not see one another throughout the following weeks. Albert began to work 'properly' in straw. Fritz certainly would have been glad to have the hard stone floor of his dark little cell made a little less hard with the aid of some straw. But he had to take things as they were. And since 'prison' was one of the signs which preceded his happy return, he remained calm and confident through all the interrogations he endured, which aimed at eliciting from him the confession that he had maltreated and killed partisans. Since he firmly repudiated every accusation, and moreover with his blue eyes and upright manner did not look like a man who would unjustly and cruelly torture and kill others, at last, with a few parting kicks, he was allowed to go. There he was again, undismayed, even though he now had a few more blue patches in addition to his blue nail. More than ever he believed in the reliability of his prophecy. What he had suffered since he had been made a prisoner! Hunger, heat, illness, and finally the uncertainty and isolation of the prison cell! But none of it had affected him. He had been, and he still was, raised above these trivialities. For he had his 'firm faith'.

It is true that there were now in the camp men who had another name for this 'firm faith'. The camp padre, a good man, but feeble and emaciated almost to skin and bones, who was able to conduct an occasional service only with the utmost effort, had spoken to the brothers several times and pointed out that they 'were assuming an enormous responsibility'. What was to happen if all these hopes, so light-heartedly awakened, were dashed, and all those who had been drawn under such a spell wakened one day to reality? For this was not faith which they had awakened and artificially nourished, but superstition and sham faith in the very worst sense. They had set up an idol which would devour them all when it saw that its hour was come—unless in good time one knocked it off its feet of clay.

The corporal had listened patiently to this. He had also answered with some pious phrases, such as 'God is behind all things', and 'Everything is ordained'. But in truth he did not understand at all. He recounted his story to everyone as before; calm and collected, he stroked his wavy dark moustache and repeated all his 'proofs' from the past and from the present, while his comrades hung upon his words as though they were bewitched. In perfect ease and self-assurance he nodded when they asked him : 'And then, didn't she say, when the blue had gone. . . ? ' 'And what she said about the number of the working-party was absolutely right, wasn't it? . . . And then we should all get home, when you had worked in stone and straw and wood? . . . And what about the cooler, that they would let you out again. . . ? '

A few days after the corporal's release from detention, his brother Albert was brought back into the camp. He did not appear in the hut, but was taken straight from the camp gates to the cooler. Fritz Becklam heard of it almost by chance, after he had gone to bed, from one of the cooks, who in his turn had heard it from one of the German guards in the cooler. Albert had been put into the very same cell which a few days earlier had been the corporal's own unhappy lodging.

If it was true, then it was annoying. There was no joking with those gentlemen; Becklam felt a slight tremor of fear. Had he himself let fall some false or stupid word which could have brought his brother under suspicion? Or had the same swine who had framed him with the NKVD made false accusations about his brother as well? For Albert had never been anything but a service corps driver in a quite ordinary unit—what could they want to fix on him?

The corporal slid down from his palliasse and with curses forced on his boots again, which were too narrow at the toes and too wide at the heels, so that his toes were a mass of sores. He went out of the hut and slowly moved in the direction of the cooler. The moon shone garish yellow in the sky; in its cold light the bare mud huts appeared barer than ever. The barbed wire gleamed like a ghostly cobweb in which the watch-towers sat like fat and loathsome spiders awaiting their prey. Between two of the huts the German prisoners had with much love and patience planted flowers, among them the garden rocket, which now in the evening spread a honeyed scent. Becklam breathed in the intoxicating scent, brooding all the while: 'What on earth can they want with him? Albert of all people! Every single man in the camp knows how easily an innocent man can get caught up in this NKVD machine. Weren't the

Russians looking for "war criminals" on whom they could take their revenge, with a patient, fanatical, icy zeal? What if Albert instead of himself. . . ?'

He went along the wall of the centre hut. Here there were sunflowers, and a special kind of bush which shot up as quickly as weeds and had therefore to be continually pruned; he had seen it in Russia for the first time. The moon was shining so stupidly! Exactly as on that night when Nina . . . Nonsense! Push on. The sunflowers against the wall of the hut looked like little moons. The corporal slipped past the cook's quarters and then past the bath-house. His long thin shadow hastened after him. Now he stood beneath the window of the cell, which was fairly high, and barred, and in addition, since some of the panes were missing, criss-crossed with barbed wire.

His heart knocked against his ribs. True, Maria had prophesied that all would be well with him. Albert, too, and 'all others' would get home, that was also settled. But . . . but if they tried the same devilries on Albert as they had tried on him! Albert had grown weak in the last few weeks; stone-breaking in that heat and with those poor rations had not done him any good at all. He had water in the feet and pains in his arms. Let us hope they don't start starving him, beating him, let us hope——!

Quiet! Was that something moving in there? No, nothing. He would have to give a call, softly. Prophecy or no prophecy, no one liked to have anything to do with the NKVD. Even the guards, fellow-Germans, those swine, were not to be trusted. The smell of those night flowers! Pure mockery! As a child he had liked honey so much, best of all fresh from the hive, when it was still clinging to the comb. And now— licking honey was all over. Flowers like that shouldn't be planted in this wilderness. What was the use of such a scent, when the huts and the latrines stank like the plague? Funny, that a flower should begin to smell like that at night, it could make one quite sad——

Suddenly he leapt up at the window. He clutched hastily at the bars of the window and called softly through the broken panes. 'Albert! Albert! Are you there?'

And he stood beneath the window again, with thumping heart. His right hand was bleeding from the barbed wire. The moon grinned broadly and wantonly right down on the latrines. A man was creeping to the door in his shirt and pants; another moved away from the dark cavity of the door. There was always life there, even if it was a wretched and feeble life, like maggots. The poor sufferers, those with weak bladders and those with dysentery, crept between hut and latrine, backwards and forwards, backwards and forwards. And the night rockets, those little fine flowers, and on the other hand that——

'Fritz! Fritz!' came a hiss from the window above.

'Yes, Albert, is that you?'

'Yes, Fritz. Push off, old fellow.'

'What do they want from you, Albert?'

'I don't know. They haven't interrogated me yet. Go away, there's a guard here. Clear off!'

Over. The corporal went back to the hut, through the moonlight and the scent of the flowers. Past the latrine and the weary shadows, going in and out with their need. None took any notice of him. He wrapped a rag round his bleeding hand, lay down and went to sleep.

Everything happened as it must.

Chapter Five

FROM THIS TIME, evening after evening, the corporal crept up to the cell window; but he could not establish any further contact with his brother. After about a week a prisoner whom he did not know came up to him and asked him softly, with his hand over his mouth: 'Are you Fritz Becklam?'

'Yes, what do you want?' replied the corporal, and scrutinized his questioner, who looked very broken down. He was reduced to mere skin and bones, his eyes were almost lifeless, and beneath them were shadows such as are seen on the face of a dying man. His face was distorted in a meek, spiritless grin, and this grin was the most pitiful thing of all.

'Your brother sent me to you,' the man went on in feeble, cracked tones, blinking at Becklam with his lifeless eyes. 'I was in the cells along with him.'

'What do you want?' repeated Becklam suspiciously.

'They are at him. Night after night.'

'What for?'

'What for!' grinned the man, swaying on his feeble legs like a caricature of death.

'Come with me,' said Becklam harshly.

They left the hut and stood outside in the shadows, looking around cautiously, as though they planned some crime.

'Have you anything to eat?' asked the ghostly creature. 'Man, they starve you.' And again that meek, spiritless grin.

'You can get something afterwards,' said Becklam, looking away from the skeleton-like figure. He suddenly thought of his brother. Now he, too, was sitting in the cell, pressing both hands on his stomach. 'What is wrong with my brother? Tell me, man!'

'What do I know? He says he is supposed to have harried and killed partisans. But he says it's not true. But they will soften him up all right. They managed it with me. . . .'

'Have they beaten him?' asked Becklam.

'I don't know. He doesn't speak about it. But he won't keep it up for long,' grinned the man. 'No matter how innocent you are. . . . I think they are mistaking him for someone else. That's the worst thing that can happen to you with the Russians.'

'What cell is he in now?' the corporal wanted to know.

'It changes. It all depends. Just as the fancy takes them. But if he remains obstinate they won't let him out of solitary confinement at all.'

'Are you certain that they are handling him . . . instead of someone else?' asked the corporal. And he was suddenly seized with hatred for the grinning, exposed skull, the inflamed and blinking eyes, the hollow cheeks and the frightful lines of pain running

61

from nose to mouth, which looked as though they were engraven by death itself. He could have plunged his fist in the poor, ruined face.

'I know nothing definite. I wish I had said nothing,' croaked the man. 'I only meant well. Don't get into a stew, man. After you've been four weeks in there, you don't know what you're saying. In the end you sign everything they put in front of you, just to make an end of it all——'

'Come with me!' said the corporal again.

And they went together to the cook-house, first past the garden rockets, whose honey scent was still not quite over, along the side of the latrines, where the sick, weary life would not give in, past the parade ground and so to the cook-house. Behind the cook-house the corporal told the man to wait. He himself went to one of the cooks and asked him for help. This was how it was. His brother was in the cells.

But the cooks were very busy at that time. As they went on with their work they said, 'Well, what about it? Getting locked up is easy here. And it doesn't matter to you two. You know in any case that you'll be home by Christmas time. What are we to say to that?'

Becklam felt offended; he himself did not know the reason. At last one of the cooks, half laughing, gave him a piece of bread. The corporal passed it on to the messenger from the cells and was glad to be rid of the fellow. These stupid cook-house *wallahs*! So long as you had stories to tell them they made you welcome. Then of their grace and mercy they gave you more than you needed; as if you were a fool whom they entertained for a joke! But now when you were really in need they began to laugh and had no time and had nothing to do with you. That was what men were like!

And now he stood once more beneath the cell window and called his brother's name. 'Albert! Albert!'

Again no sound. He seized the bar of the window and raised himself up. The barbs of the wire tore his hands; the pain was fearful, but he clung on, and called again into the window: 'Albert! Albert!'

He heard a whisper inside and a lively murmur, followed at once by a loud voice from deeper in the prison. 'What the devil's going on there?'

Fritz Becklam dropped down again. He was frightened. As he moved on he wiped the blood from his hands. In the cobblers' hut light was still burning. He entered. That was the good thing, that he was welcome everywhere with his stories. Everyone was glad to see him, especially those in the small rooms, who were bored in the evenings and needed something to cheer them up and tickle their fancy. It was certainly very late. They were all off to bed save one, and he was the very one who had never wanted to hear anything of Becklam's stories. This one cobbler, Ewald Mette by name, a Saxon from the Erzgebirge, was sitting at his low work-table, peaceful and calm, and looking at a few photographs which were spread out on the table before him. He had thin fair hair, and a firm, round face; his red snub nose gave him a happy and even comic appearance. When he stood up you could see that he

63

had a strong and very squat short upper body and was almost a hunchback. But perhaps that came from his sedentary life.

The corporal greeted him, and looked around questioningly.

'Did you want to speak to someone?' asked Mette in a friendly voice. 'They're all asleep.'

'Oh, let it pass,' growled Becklam. 'Have you some water there?'

Mette stood up. 'For drinking?' Then he saw Becklam's bleeding hand and asked: 'Now what's happened?'

The corporal only shrugged his shoulders; the other did not pursue his questioning. He brought water in a bowl, and a piece of white linen with which he bandaged the corporal's hand. Then he sat down again before his photographs. The cobblers' work-tables were tidy. In the corners great heaps of broken-down shoes were piled, on the walls here and there were pictures of women and children. It was quite different in here from the huts, it was beautifully quiet and peaceful. 'Are these your children?' asked Becklam.

'Yes,' replied the cobbler. 'This little girl here will soon be eight. And the boy was six to-day, if he's still alive.'

'Oh, he'll be alive all right,' said Becklam. 'And is that your wife?'

'Yes, that's my wife,' answered the cobbler. 'That *was* my wife. Whether she's still alive . . .'

'But of course she'll still be alive,' rejoined the corporal. 'Why shouldn't she be?'

'The one is as likely as the other,' said the cobbler meditatively. 'She was in *Silesia*, with her parents, when the Russians broke through there. Well, it'll soon be clear, one way or the other. Are you married too, Becklam?'

'No, but it's been prophesied that I shall marry a girl of our village just after I get home again. From the description she must be a farmer's daughter who lives a bit outside the village, and has a fine place with a chicken farm. She would suit me very well.'

'Oh, you and your prophecies!' said the cobbler quietly. 'How did you start on that tripe?'

'One calls it tripe and another calls it something else,' said the corporal, somewhat offended. 'At any rate, so far everything has come to pass.'

'Well, and if it has,' said the cobbler, looking attentively at the corporal's torn hand. 'What do you get out of it, that's what I'd like to know?'

'What do I get out of it?' Becklam gesticulated violently with his bandaged hand. 'I think of the future and I am at ease, because I know what will come. That's what I get out of it! What a silly question!'

But this did not seem to impress the cobbler either. 'I, too, think of the future and am at ease,' he said, 'but without the help of your silly soothsaying. Is it really true that they've brought Albert back and are interrogating him?'

The corporal nodded sullenly.

'Was that prophesied to you as well?' asked the cobbler. 'I mean, about your brother?'

'Not directly. She only said that I should be locked up, and after that, by Christmas, I and my brother should go home.'

'And if you don't go? What then?'

'We *shall* go,' replied the corporal. 'You can be sure of that.'

'I see. So that would be your last piece of wisdom: "we *shall* go". And if you don't go, in spite of everything? You're like God, you two. You know what will happen. But woe to you if it turns out differently. Then it will appear who has made fools of you. Fritz, Fritz, I tell you I have been watching for a long time. You have done a lot of damage already. You have destroyed the little scrap of true faith which many of the men had, and now——'

'True faith! What do you mean, "true faith"? The main thing is that the men have something to hold on to.'

'No. That is not the main thing,' contradicted the cobbler in a sudden wave of excitement. 'They must have a faith which even in misery . . . Everything else is no faith at all. Do you understand what I mean? They must know that God is working in our soul at the very time when we think He has forsaken us. That's the point.'

'It's possible to believe in God, even so,' persisted Becklam.

The cobbler let out his breath heavily once or twice, then he went on more calmly: 'You don't believe in God. You believe in your prophetess. And you will live to see where that lands you. And not you alone, that's the bad thing. What can we do for your brother?' he added.

'Nothing, I think.' The corporal stood up. His mood was now completely spoiled. This fellow was worse than a parson. . . .

The cobbler accompanied him in a friendly way to the door, and outside he said again: 'If I can do anything for your brother, Fritz. . . . Perhaps we can get him something to eat?'

Chapter Six

BUT THE WEEKS went by, and the corporal did not see his brother. The man from the cells now and then shuffled past him. He blinked humbly at him; the sad grin seemed to be frozen on his face for ever. He did not address the corporal; but every time Becklam saw the figure of misery, the man broken in body and spirit, he was pierced to the heart, for he thought that from day to day his brother must become more like this man.

Again and again he was drawn to the window of the cell, although he no longer dared to call in through it. Once or twice he even stole into the prison, as though making for the clothing store, which was in the same hut. He saw the doors leading to the separate cells. And while he cast a timid glance (for the guards and that devil the interpreter had their room immediately adjoining) he thought: ' Here in one of these dark holes he crouches on the ground, hour upon hour, minute upon minute. He is hungry, his thoughts torment him. He no longer knows what to say when they question him about me.'

And all at once he found it impossible to understand how all this could go on side by side: the man there in the dark hole, tormented by fleas and bugs, deprived of all power of resistance by hunger and by his own thoughts; and alongside him life in the hut, in the cook-house, the bawling of the Russians in the passing trucks on the road outside, and further off the life of the world—men and women in elegant restaurants, music and danc-ing couples. He could not understand how the sea at home could now be throwing wave after wave upon the beach, that bathing-huts were perhaps there again, and people were bathing. And here an innocent man was sitting, unable to move.

At last he shook it all off like a bad dream: 'By Christmas it will all be over. At Christmas we are going home. Maria prophesied it. Thank God. So far, everything had come to pass. This, too, will come to pass. Albert knows it, too. He will stick it out.'

And so, in spite of everything, he continued to play the 'penguin'. He said to everyone who would listen that his brother was just laughing at the Russians and at the cells. His brother knew as well as he, Fritz Beck-lam, did, that this time of suffering, too, had to come, but that it would soon be over, and despite death and the devil the brothers Becklam would go home before Christmas. He still found enough people in the camp to accept his tidings joyfully, especially when the blue on his thumb nail now clearly began to grow out and disappear. Moreover, a week before, he had been allocated to a carpenter as his assistant. There it could be clearly seen again: stone, straw, wood. It was true that only Albert had had to do with straw 'properly', but one could not be as precise as that.

Nevertheless, something was going awry. Something or other was not in order. The corporal's self-assurance was laid on too thick. Many of the men could no longer stand his garrulity and his almost feverish self-assertion and dogmatism.

At the end of August, after a long interval, another transport of sick left the camp for home; a few hundred men, all physical and mental wrecks, looking in their Hungarian jackets, their Russian summer trousers and their white sabots as though they were going to take part in a ghostly masquerade of the half-starved. The brothers Becklam were not on the list; the corporal only proclaimed the louder that this marked the beginning of the releases he had spoken of. August and half of September went past, then one evening Fritz Becklam heard the news that his brother had been sent direct from the cells to the camp hospital.

'Yes,' the medical orderly said, 'it's true. But don't come until it's dark. The Russian doctors are away then. Visiting the sick isn't allowed, you know. Three minutes, no longer.'

About twenty beds with blue check covers were crowded together in the darkening room. As the corporal looked round for his brother, one of the sick in the corner raised a hand. It was Albert. Was it really he? Dear God, it was that very face of misery which he had so feared to see!

He went up to his brother's bed, reached for his thin hand, and: 'Well, what have you been playing at, Albert?' he asked.

He said this because at the moment he could think

of nothing else to say. Albert did not raise his head, probably because he was too weak for the exertion; but he responded feebly to the handclasp and turned his face to his brother. Two or three of his teeth were missing. His moustache had also been removed, so that his emaciated, hollow face with its terrible sunken eyesockets seemed at once older and younger, with the face of an old man or the face of a boy.

'Dropsy,' was all Albert said. 'Up to the stomach.' He had the same voice as the man who had been his messenger from the cells a few weeks before. All dystrophics had the same voice.

'Now, then,' said the corporal encouragingly, 'in a few weeks we'll have you on your feet again.'

Albert moved his head on the pillow. There was doubt in the gesture.

'And at Christmas we shall both go home,' Fritz went on, 'whatever Ivan does about it!'

Albert made no reply. But he gave his brother a long, grave look. From the opposite corner a moaning arose. Someone said: 'At home the vintage will soon begin. Oh, to get home now! This would be the right time, chaps!' And immediately the moaning began again, and another voice said: 'Call the orderly, somebody! That fellow there is finished.'

Then Albert said softly: 'Perhaps we shall not go home either, Fritz.'

'Why not?' The corporal was almost enraged. 'Heavens above, I am now working on the Finnish houses. You remember: "neither house nor tent". That, too, has come to pass like everything else.'

'But perhaps the very last thing of all will not come to pass,' said Albert, and in his croaking voice there could be heard a strange resolution.

'Albert, man!' The corporal searched for words. 'It is as sure as the Amen in church.'

Albert's glance, which was tired but not yet quite extinguished, turned to the window, beyond which a few solitary tiny stars could be seen. He said towards the window and the stars: 'Leave the Amen in church out of it, Fritz.'

The corporal sat down on the edge of his brother's bed, although his three minutes must have been long over.

'Don't talk nonsense, Albert,' he said, and lowered his voice, as though he were uttering some frightful blasphemy. 'Don't talk nonsense. They have brought you to such a state that you cannot believe any more——'

'No, no, Fritz, they haven't brought me to such a state,' said the sick man, interrupting him. 'They have not done it by a long chalk. I can still believe, Fritz. Perhaps more than before. Only I don't believe any more that we shall go home at Christmas.'

'Well, and when, if not then?' asked the corporal.

'I don't know. Only one knows that. One single one. That's enough for me.'

'But not for me,' said the corporal hotly. 'If everything so far has come to pass——'

'Oh, stop it, Fritz!' interrupted Albert again in vexation. His glance still rested on the few tiny stars beyond the window. He had not seen them for so long a time in his pitch-black cell. After a time he went

72

on more calmly: 'Dear Fritz, when you cower there in that dark hole day upon day, week upon week, month upon month, and when you don't have a soul left who can help you, and from day to day you become weaker and your legs get thicker and . . . and . . . well, anyway, what is left to you in the end but to say, "Dear God, you know." And if to-day I should close my eyes, what does it profit me that everything was prophesied aright . . . except the very last thing? But that I can rely on my God, Fritz, that He . . . that He waits for me. . . .'

The corporal wriggled impatiently on the edge of the bed. 'You *must* get home, Albert. You have a wife and a child and parents. Have you forgotten all that?'

The sick man compressed his lips. And only after a long time he replied, almost in a whisper. 'Forgotten? Man, what do you imagine I have been thinking about, day and night, in that dark hole? Day and night? . . . What will you do, Fritz, when everything collapses over you, one day? Am I better than the other hundred thousand who will not get home, either? Can I pull myself together more than I am doing? For my wife and child things will——'

The orderly stuck his head excitedly in at the door. 'Get out, quick, Becklam! The Russian M.O.'s here. Fool. Didn't I say three minutes? But that's like you all. I am good-hearted, and you take advantage. If I'm put on the spot because of you, you——!'

The corporal was in low spirits. He felt a queer pain round his stomach; but it was not hunger; a short time before he had had a bowlful of soup from one of the cooks, though accompanied by the humiliating warning that he must not hang about the cook-house so much. So it was not hunger. It was something else. . . . The corporal's thoughts turned involuntarily to the evening with the cobbler. It was as though the cobbler and his brother had arranged things together! Just when it was important not to weaken!

Fritz Becklam was very fond of his brother. He was sore at heart to see Albert so ill. In the following days he went round begging for him and brought to him in the hospital whatever he could rake together—soup, bread, onions. Latterly he even went to Mette, the cobbler, and asked him: 'Ewald, have you something for Albert? He is in hospital, he's got dropsy. That's how it is.'

And the cobbler went at once to his cupboard, took out what was in it, his whole ration of bread and an onion, and said: 'Come back in an hour, Fritz. Bring your dixie-pot with you. What's the form? Is it possible to see Albert?'

'If you're on good terms with the orderly,' answered Becklam. 'He doesn't let me in now. But he takes the things you bring.'

The next evening the orderly seemed to be in a good mood.

'You can speak to him for a moment,' he said, as the corporal stood at the door with a piece of bread in his hand. 'But not too long. You can never tell. Then I get into trouble afterwards.'

When Fritz Becklam entered the sick room, he saw the cobbler sitting on Albert's bed. He went nearer,

74

and it seemed to him as though his brother now had a little more life and strength in his expression.

'How are you getting on?' he asked at once. And Albert answered: 'Very well, Fritz. And thank you for everything.'

'You're welcome,' rejoined the corporal, in the helplessly artificial manner in which simpler people try to conceal their feelings on such occasions. 'You look a great deal better than you did the other day,' he went on.

His brother exchanged a calm, long look with the cobbler, who sat on the foot of the bed.

'The interpreter has also been here, Fritz,' he answered.

'Well, and——?' A little hot fear ran through the corporal's heart. 'What did he want?'

'Oh, he wanted to see if I was on the mend,' said the sick man calmly.

'Nonsense, Albert! The prison cell is over and done with.'

Again Albert Becklam exchanged glances with the cobbler. Then he answered meditatively: 'I think it's only going to begin in real earnest now, Fritz.'

'Don't talk nonsense, Albert! What can they want from you?' But the corporal suddenly had once more that uncomfortable, queasy feeling in the pit of his stomach.

'What they want from me? Quite simple. I am supposed to have tortured and killed Russian civilians.'

'But you didn't!' burst out the corporal.

'No, I didn't,' said his brother, looking through the

75

windows to the stars. 'But others, perhaps, did do it.'

'What others?' It seemed to the corporal as though a foreigner were speaking to him in a foreign language. 'Do you think that perhaps I killed civilians?'

'Oh, no, I suppose you didn't, either. But others, perhaps. . . .'

'And you have to pay for it?'

'Yes, Fritz, I have to pay for it.'

'But that's pure madness, Albert!' cried the corporal. 'Who has talked you into that?' And he cast a furious glance at the cobbler, sitting quietly there with his red nose and his short, fat neck, as though the conversation were about nothing in particular.

'No one has talked me into it,' answered his brother. 'And I haven't asked for it, either—all that I have to go through.'

'Well, then! That's what I meant.' The corporal became slowly calmer. 'See here, it may be another six weeks, and then the blue will be out of my nail. And then the time has come for us both.'

The cobbler and Albert glanced at the nail; but with a look of indifference, almost of scorn.

After a while the cobbler gave a slight sigh, and said: 'No, no one asks for what he has to go through. You can learn that here. But you must take it *as though* you had asked for it.'

It annoyed the corporal that the two of them had scarcely deigned to look at his thumb nail. 'But if you are innocent, what then?' he cried.

'Innocent!' said the cobbler, in the same thoughtful

76

tone. 'My dear Fritz, who of us is innocent? You perhaps? Have you never in your life done anything evil?' He rose, and reached for his cap: then he gazed reflectively first at the sick man and then at the corporal, as though awaiting an answer.

It was almost dark in the bare, low room. From outside could be heard the indistinct and wretched sounds of the camp orchestra holding a 'social evening' in the open air. A thin, nasal tenor sang 'O maiden, my maiden, how I love thee'. The medical orderly looked in. 'Some stupid swine has been smoking again, damn you. And you two, clear off! How long do you expect to sit around?'

A timid voice was heard: 'Orderly, have you nothing for headaches?'

'And now you!' said the orderly roughly. 'Why didn't you open your mouth earlier, when the doctor was here? Do you think I can whistle them up out of my belly?'

Outside the hut the cobbler and the corporal stood together for a while in silence, before they went on their way. The stars were brighter now in the pale blue evening sky. The five or six musicians of the camp orchestra had settled down in a sheltered spot between the two main huts, a great crowd of the men were standing or sitting around them, listening with resignation, their faces lifeless, to the sounds which recalled better times; what was happening was like a pitiful parody of what life had once been. As the corporal and the cobbler approached, they heard a compère producing his sad jokes. He addressed his comrades in misery as 'Gentle-

77

men'. After every joke he gave an affected bow: and was probably thinking of the mouthful of soup which he hoped to earn by his wretched masquerade.

'Do you really believe that they will fetch him away again, once he's better?' asked the corporal.

'Yes,' said the cobbler. 'I believe they will.'

'The devil take them!' exploded Becklam. 'That is the absolute dead end.' After a time he continued in a changed voice: 'Listen, Ewald, it almost seems to me —how can I put it—he seems so changed. . . . I once heard that a man—if he is so long in solitary confinement . . .'

'That he goes out of his mind, you mean?' the cobbler finished his sentence for him. 'No, don't give yourself any anxiety on *that* score, Fritz. Don't give yourself any anxiety.'

'But you can say what you like,' persisted Becklam. 'He's not the same as he was before.'

'That may be true,' admitted the cobbler reflectively, and more to himself than to Becklam. 'That is to say, he has grasped . . . grasped—no, if I am worried about anyone, Fritz,' he went on aloud, 'then it's you, and not your brother. Your brother has won through. But you are ruining yourself. Remember what I say, and think of me. You have still not learned a thing. If you don't learn soon, it will be too late. Good night, Fritz.'

The corporal went nearer to the music. But now they were breaking up. At the camp gate the signal for lights-out was sounding. A shrill note of iron on iron, almost like a bell. But it was only an old piece of railway line which hung there. The men slowly shuffled

78

away. Most of them went first to the latrines before going to their huts. The stars grew steadily brighter in the sky. Somewhere far away, shrill, very loud women's voices were singing a song in several parts. A man passing the corporal looked up and said in a tired voice: 'The steppes are howling to-night.' But it was a beautiful song which the shrill voices were singing far away. It really did sound as though the absorbing spaces of Russia were raising their solitary voice.

The corporal did not want to make for his hut just yet. He had a sudden fear of the hot smell which would meet him there like the blow of a fist. Nor was he properly finished with all that he had heard that day. That they had suddenly ceased to believe in what was as clear as day! The very night before, he had received a new sign that gave new nourishment and hope to himself and to all who believed in his prophecy. Maria had prophesied to him—he had almost forgotten—that his last delousing would take place after midnight, and moreover on a Friday. On the Thursday evening at ten o'clock he was summoned to the bath-house along with his brigade. 'Just watch this,' he had said to his comrades. 'My delousing won't happen till after midnight.' His comrades had laughed and said that he had miscalculated this time. He was already standing naked, and was just being sent into the barbers' room, when the chief appeared and explained that there would be a delay, as there was something wrong with his stove. And so it came about that the corporal and his comrades were not deloused till two a.m. . . . Did anyone dare to say now that the whole thing was quite ordinary?

Chapter Seven

ON OCTOBER 20 the interpreter took Albert Becklam back to the cells. Two days before, he had been released from the hospital, still rather weak and thin but nevertheless 'able to get around'. His bed was not beside his brother's again, but in the hut reserved for those unfit for work. When the corporal went to his hut after work, in order to take him to the sports ground (that was the best place for an undisturbed talk), he had gone.

'What's up? Where's my brother?' he asked the man who was lying next to Albert's empty place. But in fact he knew already where his brother was.

The man turned slowly round to him. He was smoking, but everything he did was in slow motion, he was so weak; slowly he raised the cigarette to his mouth, slowly he sucked in the smoke, slowly there formed deep cavities in his cheeks. . . . His clouded, tired eyes gazed at the questioner, and he seemed to make a great effort to think. Then he replied: 'Gone. Taken away. This morning.'

'Who? Who, then?' The corporal felt that he could not produce a longer intelligible sentence than that.

The man on the bed grinned, in slow motion. Slowly his lips parted, slowly countless folds and wrinkles formed on his wizened face. 'NKVD,' was all he said. But the way he said it contained everything: horror, scorn, awe, mockery. 'NKVD,' he repeated after a while, turning his gaze on the corporal with a great effort.

'But why?' asked Becklam—quite senselessly, for how was the poor wretch to know? Nor did he await an answer, but asked another question: 'What did he say when they took him away? Were you there?'

'Say? Nothing,' replied the man, and slowly the corners of his mouth dropped. 'What is a man to say when he's taken away? He just nodded, like this . . . look here . . . nodded like this. And then he packed his things. And then he went with them. Out there, through the door.'

'How did he look?' was Becklam's next question.

'How did he look? Nothing particular. He wasn't exactly laughing. But he . . .'

'Was he frightened?'

'Frightened? Perhaps. Probably. . . . Nobody likes to have to do with those gentlemen. No, there was not much to notice about him. Only his hands trembled a little.'

'Did he leave any message for me?'

'No. Oh, yes, he did. His best wishes. That was all.'

The corporal turned to go. Then he noticed that the man on the bed was blinking at him in a covert, foolish, consequential manner. His head was twitching as with someone who wants to make a confidential sign; but since this, too, went in slow motion, the whole effect was ridiculous and incomprehensible, but at least seemed to indicate that the dystrophic wanted to ask the corporal something particular. But when Becklam did turn to him to listen, the man on the palliasse whispered in his ear with his hoarse, attenuated voice: ' Is it true that we are all going to get home? All of us? The sick as well? Is it really prophesied? '

Suddenly the corporal felt an ugly and furious loathing for the man on the palliasse, although all the man wanted to hear from him was what he had hitherto been only too willing to tell to everyone who would listen. He could have swept the man off his bed, he was so consumed by fury and by a burning misery. He replied with a gesture which expressed, to the astonishment of the questioner, all these sensations; then he turned hastily away and left the hut. But outside he halted in utter confusion of spirit. Dear God, now the misery was beginning all over again. Now the poor wretch was sitting once more in his dark hole, hungry, a martyr to his thoughts, and freezing besides, for in the unheated cell it was, of course, cold. . . . The corporal began to walk, to walk fast, for no other reason than not to have to stand still. He went round the sports ground once, twice, until he had become somewhat calmer. By that time he had pulled himself together enough to be able to say to himself: ' We shall be home by Christmas! We shall be home by Christmas! '

Fine. But if only Albert could believe it as well.

82

Then everything would be easier for him. Then everything would be . . . And he moved towards the cells; as though under compulsion. One of the prison guard, gross and overfed, was slouching in the outer entrance. This man, the spy of the NKVD, was scarcely less hated and feared than the interpreter. Everyone avoided him or else sought by some means to win his favour. Fritz Becklam saw the man standing before his brother's prison, and felt a passionate desire to knock him down with his bare fists. Rage, hate and scorn gleamed in his eyes as he shouted at the well-fed creature: 'Is my brother there again—in there?'

The guard blinked a little, then mumbled through his teeth: 'Move on there, you scum!'

'You must tell me if you've shut my brother up again!' cried the corporal. At that moment it was all one to him, it would have been sheer pleasure to thrash the other man or to be thrashed by him.

But the guard—he was a German from Galicia and had once been a decent N.C.O. in the German Army —only grinned impudently: '"You,"' he said condescendingly, 'what do you mean—"You"? I don't shut anyone up. I simply watches out that no one gets away.'

'Then is my brother in again? Yes or no?'

The German shrugged his shoulders ever so slightly. 'Must ask the NKVD, not me.'

The corporal turned and went away. His anger had disappeared, and all that was left was the burning misery, a nagging and consuming anxiety.

Ewald Mette was not in his workshop. A few other

cobblers invited the corporal to come in and talk about the journey home. When they noticed that he was in low spirits and discovered the reason, they said in loud and jovial tones: 'What of it? If you are both going home at Christmas all the same, what does a little stretch in the cells matter?' And they slapped Becklam on the shoulder and regaled him with bread and coffee (for the cobblers had almost always something in their cupboard); and when he left their workshop he himself believed that he had been wrong to worry. He had once more become the 'penguin'. Nothing could happen to him or to his brother. The bad times just had to be endured, and that was that.

Ten days later he met his brother in the camp road, just as he was being taken by the interpreter for inter-rogation. It was early evening. The corporal was returning with his party from work; he was shuffling along in the crowd of men, thinking of nothing; moving with the stream which was pouring from the camp gates to the huts. Fritz Becklam was tired; his gaze was fixed dully on his feet, and he only looked up as he came to the door of his hut. At that moment he saw his brother, perhaps ten steps away. Albert was walking slowly in front of the flat-footed interpreter, who was circling round him like a dog. He dragged his legs heavily, as though in his cell he had half-forgotten how to walk. The corporal was horrified to see how leaden-grey his brother's face had become; his cheeks, swollen with hunger-oedema, were hanging loosely down. On his face and upper lip was a black stubble which gave him an appearance of disorder and wildness. But his brother's

84

look was, neveretheless, of a heart-rending, mild clarity, like the look of a child. Of course he had sat so long in the dark that he was rejoicing in the daylight. But how painfully he dragged his legs, how weakly his arms dangled by his side! And that stubble, and those loose pouches on his face, full of dropsy, dancing up and down with every step. Oh, dear God, how he swayed along past the swarm of prisoners, who looked at him sideways, shyly and nervously, as though he were outcast, a victim of the plague! How that watchdog, that flat-footed cur of an interpreter, circled the humbled and terribly broken man!

And now Albert had caught sight of his brother. Painfully he opened his eyes wide, blinked, and smiled. He opened his mouth and said, but inaudibly: 'Fritz.'

The corporal went as close to his brother's side as he could and said under his breath: 'How are you, Albert?'

And he saw that his brother answered him. Perhaps he said 'Well'. It must have been something of the sort. Yes, he definitely said 'Well', and he was smiling all the time: he was so pleased to meet his brother once again, even though the next moment the watchdog, the interpreter, had pushed him on and away. Fritz remained standing there, and watched his brother until he had disappeared round the corner. How he dragged his legs!

The corporal went to get his meal. After that he got the order to collect warm clothes from the store for his brigade; and when at last he was free he stationed himself on the road again and waited for the interpreter to

85

bring his brother back to the cells. He waited an hour, two hours. The autumn stars were visible once more in their indifferent cold beauty above the hutted town. From time to time there swelled up, from some part of the wide countryside beyond, or from the huts where the Russian workers were quartered, a loud part-song, as though born out of the heart of the night, rising out of the depths of the earth, full of melancholy and plaintive desire. But still Albert did not return. Perhaps he was long since back in his dark, cold hole. The corporal stood beneath the barred window. Before it a withered little tree swayed in the wind. The prisoners themselves had planted it there the previous year, and now, like everything in the camp, it was slowly fading away. There was room for real anxiety about Albert now. He had looked like someone who expected nothing more. At least in this life. That anyone could rejoice as he did over that wretched bit of daylight!

The cobbler Mette came at once to the door when Fritz Becklam called his name. 'Yes, I know,' he said, and his head sank between his round shoulders. 'They have interrogated him again. There's nothing to be done about it. They try again and again.'

They went past the latrine, on to the dark sports ground. They halted behind the equipment store. Here the wind did not blow so cold, and it was also possible to speak without being overheard.

'But in heaven's name, what is it they really want of him?' cried the corporal.

'What they want of him?' The cobbler thoughtfully tapped out his home-made pipe and looked long and speculatively at his excited companion.

'Yes! They can't lock up a man and let him starve in a dark hole for nothing at all. They must have some purpose, something definite.'

The cobbler waited almost in astonishment till the corporal's rage was exhausted, then said, a little exasperated: 'Do you really not know what's going on?'

And when the corporal made a gesture, which might have meant anything or nothing: 'Then I'll tell you,' Mette went on. 'It's really you they're after. Someone has informed on you. It's you that the whole thing's about, not your brother. They know that one of you has harried partisans. It was you, wasn't it?'

'Yes, but . . . they couldn't prove it.'

'Right. Now they're proving it was your brother. In their own way. They think your brother is the criminal.'

'Criminal? How? And what if I did harry partisans? What's the crime in that? Didn't we have to protect ourselves from those scoundrels who ambushed and tortured and mutilated our comrades? What was it but self-defence, even when we hanged one of them now and then?'

The cobbler nodded sadly.

'The Russians see the thing differently. They only see that some of their people have been hanged. They've won the war and we have lost it. Now their partisans are heroes because they killed us. And we are criminals because we killed their partisans. That's how it goes in the world.'

87

'But am I to go up,' Becklam shouted indignantly, 'am I to go up and say: "Punish me, I am a war criminal! I have defended myself against your treacherous partisans"?'

'They want their revenge, Fritz. And Albert has to be a sacrifice, even though he has never had to do with these things. So far as I know, he was a cook in a reserve unit.'

'No, God knows, he has never harmed a fly,' agreed the corporal. 'He is as innocent as anyone can be.'

They were silent for a while. In the nearby shunting-yard a Russian locomotive was whistling so loudly and continuously that it was impossible to hear oneself speaking. Not far from them, on the other side of the barbed wire, two Russian guards went past with a watchdog. One of them was singing quietly to himself.

'The stupid thing,' the cobbler resumed, 'is that they don't believe him. Perhaps he didn't shake his head energetically enough when they began. Or he was uncertain, since he knew that it was you they meant. Or . . . what do I know? Perhaps they know, too, that he had nothing to do with the matter, but they want —but no, I don't believe that!' he concluded, and waved the thought away with his hand.

'What? What do they want?' the corporal asked excitedly.

'Oh, I only thought . . . perhaps they want to see if you will come forward of your own accord and try to get your brother out of the mess.'

'Nonsense! How can I do that?' The corporal was

choking with excitement. 'Do they think I shall go to them and say: "Leave my brother in peace, he has never had anything to do with partisans, take me, it was me"? Do you think I will do that?'

'No, no, of course you won't do that,' said the cobbler. (But again he looked at Becklam in the same speculative way as at the beginning of their talk.)

'If I did that I would certainly be mad!' swore the corporal. 'Just imagine it. I go up. I stand in front of the NKVD and I say: "Gentlemen, I am the crim——" pure madness, I tell you! Sheer suicide!'

'Yes, probably,' the cobbler agreed quietly; he had begun to fill his pipe again.

'Or how do you see it?' The corporal was still not pacified. 'Ewald, man, tell me quite candidly, how do you see it?' And when the cobbler did not answer, he went on: 'They must let him go again when they can't prove anything against him. It would be against all law and justice. They *must* let him go again!'

'It doesn't look as if they will,' said the cobbler.

'We'll see about that!' said the corporal defiantly.

They went back to the hut. Above them a shooting-star drew a brilliant white line across the sky.

At the latrine they stopped again, and the corporal began afresh: 'Do you think they will really soften Albert up? So that he says something about me?'

'No. He would sooner die.'

'Well, then,' Becklam reflected. 'He must just endure a little longer, then he'll be free and everything will be right. But if I go to them now and stand in for him and incriminate myself, that doesn't at all mean

89

that he'll be free. But it would certainly mean that I would be finished. Well, what am I to do?'

'It's hard to advise,' said the cobbler.

'One would like to help, but one can't,' explained the corporal, and now his voice sounded depressed. 'The one thing's as bad as the other.'

'You see!' assented the cobbler. 'Thank heaven, that at last you . . . You thought before that nothing could happen to you, with your prophesyings!'

'I still think that,' said the corporal hotly. 'Albert and I will be home by Christmas. You can take my word for that. In six weeks all this will be forgotten.'

'Just take care that you're not forgotten yourself,' said the cobbler angrily. 'Just take care that you—oh, what's the use!'

He waved his pipe violently, settled his head down between his fat shoulders and turned away.

Chapter Eight

FROM THAT TIME the corporal began to live a kind of double life. During the day and also at the evening meal he played the 'penguin', even though his plumage was no longer so sleek and clean as it had been in White Russia. When the rumour went round the camp that the Russians were preparing a new transport home for November, he spoke of it as though it were, so to say, all his own work. Solemnly and presumptuously he boasted that by Christmas 'everyone' would be home, especially his brother Albert, who, it was true, was still languishing in prison, but would soon laugh at the Russians. And there were still many who listened to his words only too eagerly, who listened all the more eagerly as the anxious fear deepened in their hearts that their imprisonment was going from bad to worse, and that the worst sufferings and the most malicious surprises were still in store for them.

But even though the corporal reiterated to himself and others a hundred times a day that he was not wrong and that everything was in order and would soon be over now, by night he was driven by a tormenting power, when he was unable to speak to others and tell them of his 'faith'.

91

Since that time he had seen the cobbler Mette only once, one evening when he was creeping as usual to the detention hut. It was then that he became properly undeceived about the cobbler, and he resolved to have nothing more to do with the fellow. For the cobbler was coming straight from the cells : that was quite clear. But to Becklam's question where he had come from, he only replied : ' Albert's bad, you know that? '

' Really? How do you know? ' asked the corporal.

' I know. You can believe me.'

' You can only have heard that from the guards.'

' It doesn't matter where I heard it. But he's bad, and he must get out of that cold hole immediately.'

' Get him out yourself, if you can ! ' The corporal was roused.

' I can't do it. I would if I could,' said the cobbler.

' Well? Can *I* do it? '

' Everything possible must be done, Fritz. The Russians must understand that he is the wrong man.'

' They must understand ! What rubbish you talk ! The Russians don't understand anything. It would be absolute madness for me to go to them. I told you that before. And besides——'

' Fritz ! ' said the cobbler, and he came up quite close to the corporal. ' Something *must* be done, even if it goes wrong. Your brother cannot stick it out any longer.'

' He just must stick it out. It's only a short time now. In a few weeks he'll be out of that hole and home. That is as certain as the Amen in——'

' Oh, stop that ! You and your Amen in church !

And make an end of this accursed prophesying which only keeps you from acting according to your conscience. I tell you, Albert must get out of that cell, or he's finished.'

'And I tell you that those who put him in must bring him out.'

'What d'you mean by that?' asked the cobbler in astonishment.

'Nothing at all.' The corporal felt that he had said something stupid and mean; but he was no longer master of what he said. So he continued, while the cobbler cast a burning look upon him: 'I mean those same people who are on good terms with the prison guards.'

The cobbler shot out his fist. At the last moment he let his arm drop; but he was terribly agitated.

'You're out of your wits,' he jerked out, almost inaudibly. He drew in deep and trembling breaths, in order to continue; but now the Russian duty officer drew near, and the men had to part.

No, the corporal wanted to have no more to do with the cobbler, with that stupid, conceited and dogmatic fellow. He shunned his presence; for there wasn't a sensible word to be heard from him.

Some days later a transport did in fact set off for home; but it consisted of just over two hundred men, all weaklings and invalids. Albert Becklam was not among them, far less Fritz.

On the evening of that day the corporal stood as usual at the entrance to the prison. Hearing voices within, he stood in the dark corner beside the door. The

93

interpreter came out with one of the guards; it was about eight o'clock, the two of them were probably going to a show put on by the theatrical group. They were laughing about something, their cigarettes were gleaming. When they had disappeared, Becklam stepped swiftly into the gloomy entrance. He could not be seen there from the guard room; but all the same his heart was thumping as though about to burst. He listened. Listened. He heard yawning; soft whistling . . . that came from the guard room. Now, now! thought the corporal. He pressed against the door of the first cell and whispered through the peep-hole: 'Albert! Albert!'

Nothing. No answer. It was the wrong cell.

The corporal was about to slink along to the next cell when he was startled and horrified to hear Albert's voice coming from the cell immediately adjoining the guard room. It was Albert's voice without any doubt, though distorted and enfeebled—the voice of an old man. But the horrible thing about this voice was that it was singing. It was singing a hymn which sounded rusty and thin and ragged, like the song of a child who is lost in the woods. Clear and painfully penetrating, it rose out of the cell, word upon word, note upon note:

> 'Oh wait, my soul, wait on the Lord,
> Commend all things to him, he loves to help,
> Be without fear, the dawn is near,
> And spring comes on winter's heels,
> In every storm and every need
> He will protect you, the true God.'

94

The corporal listened, listened. . . . And when the voice was silent, he suddenly saw Albert and himself in the square before the village school at home. Albert was two years younger, and their mother had always insisted on Fritz's taking the smaller boy by the hand on the way to school. The square before the school had always been so beautifully sunny, and in the breaks they played tig in it. Fritz Becklam also saw the teacher with his fiddle, teaching them that hymn. He had never really liked it much, perhaps because it was mostly sung at funerals.

But there was his brother's voice again, that distorted, rusty voice of an old man, which pierced his soul through and through.

'*Oh wait, my soul, wait on the Lord,*
Commend all things to him, he loves to help.
Though all things break
God does not forsake——'

And then a chair was pushed back in the guard room, there was the dull bang of a fist on the table, and a furious growl: 'Quiet! That accursed singing!'

And then quietness. Not another sound. Not another sound. The quietness of the grave. Perhaps the man in the cell blushed for shame or for grief, if he still had the strength to be ashamed or to feel grieved. The corporal slunk out like a beaten dog. Outside he stood still, utterly blind and deaf in spirit. When someone approached, someone or other who was probably just some such poor devil as himself, he quickly stumbled

95

away. In his distraction he went past the latrine, on to the sports ground, and after that up and down on the camp road, up and down, up and down.

And his brother's voice was continually in his ears, loud, terribly loud: 'Oh wait, my soul. . . . Though all things break . . .' How horribly familiar these words had suddenly become! They had slumbered in his soul more than twenty years, and now they were present again, in their somewhat cheap and sweet emphasis, and were speaking to him, to *him*: 'Be without fear, the dawn is near.' Who could endure it—this poor, enfeebled voice, praising the 'true God'! This God who let the innocent suffer and starve and freeze and reel from torment to torment. . . . 'He will protect you.' Yes, He had protected him, the poor wretch. He had protected him perhaps a hundred times, only to let him slowly perish at last in an NKVD cell! 'Oh, this accursed war!' the corporal thought, but now this did not help him in his extremity. For this time it was his own brother who was suffering and dying there. Not just some Russian or other, some little foreign Nina. Now it really was high time that the prophecy came to pass, otherwise it would be too late. It was his brother, his youngest brother, whom he loved, whose hand his mother had always put in his when they went to school. At the time when they were still children. . . .

Did the moon always shine here? Oh, the corporal hated the cold, grinning face of the moon looking down on all the misery of the huts. Every crack in the mud walls could be clearly seen, every rat which waddled out of the cesspool, satiated and at ease.

96

A cook came past, with a full bowl in his hand. His twenty-four hour shift was over and he was now going to his quarters to sleep. When he saw Becklam standing there so distractedly, he spoke to him affably: 'Now, Fritz, you old prophet. What's wrong with you to-day? Come with me and talk to me before I go to sleep!'

And he flourished his bowl as a promise.

The corporal followed him; but he had almost nothing to say. Only as he sat with the cooks, who had a room of their own and lived almost like lords, only when he had eaten, and with the encouragement of a few well-meant words had become his usual self, did he slowly resume his old 'penguin' role. When they asked him how matters stood now with the home transport of them all, he threw out his chest and explained that the blue was still not quite out of his thumb nail, as everyone could see. And if this waiting was hard for anyone then it was surely himself, for his brother was still languishing there in the cells, starving and freezing. Yes, if he didn't firmly believe that this show was not going to last more than a few weeks, perhaps only a few days, then he would be the first to go and break up the whole concern.

'That's right! That's right! Man, Becklam, you're a great chap!' the cooks shouted, half amused and half carried away by so much audacity and firmness of spirit. 'You have at least got the faith we need. You'll do it, old chap. Come here, empty the bowl! Roll yourself a cigarette!'

And so in the end they were all happy and in good

spirits about the 'firm faith' which the corporal had given them. He left the cooks' quarters; and scarcely was he alone again than his brother's dying voice sounded anew in his heart. 'Oh wait, my soul. . . . Though all things break, God does not forsake. . . .' Dear God, where was firm faith, then? thought the corporal. He shuffled through the hut, where five hundred men were breathing, speaking in their sleep, coughing, moaning. He let the close animal heat ripple comfortably through his freezing limbs, but immediately he thought of his brother in the cold cell, freezing cruelly, minute by minute. And then he lay awake for a while on his palliasse, tormented by ugly and confused thoughts. Images from his childhood swung past his mind's eye. But the hymn which his brother had sung in the cell, like the trumpet of the Last Judgement, smashed again and again the peaceful pictures of childhood: the house with the lilac trees, the horse-mill behind the barn, the stream with the ducks and the geese on it, the seat beside the door, the edge of the wood. . . . And so his dream went on. His soul had become a merry-go-round. The same pictures kept revolving round him, and a wretched creaking and whistling barrel-organ played a tune which soaked like poison into his inmost being: 'Wait, my soul, wait upon the Lord. . . . Wait, my soul, wait upon the Lord . . . wait, my soul, wait upon the Lord.'

Chapter Nine

THAT WAS IN NOVEMBER. Advent came, but with it came nothing that brought Christmas to mind, except cold, a great deal of snow, and, in the days immediately before Christmas, a few artificial Christmas trees in some of the huts.

The only thing that emerged in these weeks from the cells was a rumour that the prisoners had been given furs; and that the Jewish doctor had ordered stoves to be put into the cells. But on December 19 Fritz Becklam heard from one of the medical orderlies that Albert, suffering from severe oedema and inflammation of the lungs, had been put first into the camp hospital, and after that (since the camp medical officer did not like a prisoner to die in the camp), had been sent to the central hospital. On Christmas Eve the corporal received the news from a convalescent that his brother had died the day before. When he had arrived at the central hospital he had sent greetings to his brother, and in the delirium into which he had afterwards passed he had repeatedly called out his name, and had also babbled a kind of song; but no one had been able to recognize what song it was—probably it was not a song

99

at all. In the frenzy of fever people did all sorts of things.

Even before Fritz Becklam heard this news he was in a bad enough state. His thumb nail was now quite clean, there was not the slightest trace of blue to be seen on it, nothing at all, nothing. But neither was there the slightest trace of any transport. And he had also been again to the bath-house, before midnight, too. He was gripped by a deep and raging disillusion, and then by violent defiance, when he caught the mocking and ugly glances of the men who had trusted in his prophecy as firmly as he himself had. In those days some of them even came up to him and asked: 'Well, you darned prophet, what about that transport home now?' And many of them threatened him with a thrashing if he dared to breathe another word of his nonsense. It was also the darkest time which they had so far experienced, as in those months, as a result of the great drought in Russia, the torments of hunger and want were specially severe. The only Christmas trees were a few broomsticks with little twigs stuck in them; to look at them was a grief. In addition, many of the prisoners were kept longer than usual at their working posts on Christmas Eve. What a terrible gloom lay upon the camp on that very day which at home had always been so bright with supernatural brightness! In all this it was only natural that disillusionment about the unfulfilled prophecy should strengthen the general feeling of hopelessness and make more exquisite the torment of heart.

The corporal was not one of those who had to work longer on Christmas Eve. He sat on his bed and stared at nothing. Perhaps it was not true that Albert was dead? How often one heard that people had died in the central hospital, and afterwards they turned up merrily as convalescents in the camp. But then he thought of his brother's singing in the cell, he thought of that rusty, thin, frail, old man's voice which came as from the grave; and he knew that Albert was dead. He saw him before his eyes, not among the living but among the dead. The dead could look so strange; one did not recognize many of them in death, especially those fallen in war or by violence. The starved, too, had such a strange look. Albert had really been a stranger from the time he met him on the camp road. And when he sang . . . The corporal stood up and left the hut.

It was snowing, with thick, cold flakes. The snow was already lying knee-deep; the wretched shovelling of snow would undoubtedly begin again in their free time. Fritz Becklam shambled towards the latrine, as always when he was at his wits' end. There, too, it was cold, the snow was seeping in a fine powder through the leaky roof. From the latrine he went to the prison hut. Only when he was standing beneath the barred window, with cold feet—for his shoes were as usual in pieces—did he remember that Albert was no longer there. Who knows, they had probably buried him by now. Then he must lie beneath the earth now, of course without a coffin. What did one say in the army? 'He sees the potatoes from underneath.' God, it all happens so quickly with a man. To-day he is flushed with life, to-morrow . . . No, the poor fellow had not been flushed for many a long day. And now he was—what had Maria said? 'Free.' Yes, he was free, free of everything.

Suddenly the corporal was standing before the cobblers' quarters. If he was not mistaken they were singing a carol inside. He stepped into the corridor, listened. Yes, they were singing 'Still the night, holy the night'. The corporal leaned back against the wall. He listened intently. They were singing loud and strong; he thought he could feel the mud walls and the mud floor trembling under the impact of sound. He reached out for the latch of the door. He suddenly felt terribly homesick. A deep and nameless misery penetrated to the very depths of his heart; he no longer knew what he ought to do. Suddenly he was overwhelmed by a gnawing, horrible hunger; as though his bowels were beginning to howl. He opened the door and went in. Ten or fifteen men were sitting in a circle round a real little Christmas tree. On it burned a few candles which were obviously home-made, for they burnt dully and gave out more smoke than light.

Not one of the men turned to look at the incomer. They were all looking at the little tree with its lights, a strange and utterly remote brilliance in their eyes. But Ewald Mette, the cobbler, had noticed the corporal. He looked at him and gave him a nod, almost startled by his appearance. For Becklam was standing stiff as a rod beside the door, his face rigid and embittered. Nor did he respond to the cobbler's nod, but stood as though on the point of leaving—as though he expected to be thrown out at once.

When the carol was over the cobbler stood up, raised

a little open book close to his eyes, and in his peaceful country voice read slowly and clearly, like a child in school:

> '*In the beginning was the Word, and the Word was with God, and the Word was God.*
>
> *The same was in the beginning with God.*
>
> *All things were made by him; and without him was not anything made that was made.*
>
> *In him was life; and the life was the light of men.*
>
> *And the light shineth in darkness; and the darkness comprehended it not.*'

Darkness fell upon the corporal's eyes. From hunger and from that terrible burning misery, which had overwhelmed him since midday. The lights on the Christmas tree, the venerable words of the gospel were no comfort, they only increased his sufferings. But the cobbler was reading on:

> '*He came unto his own, and his own received him not.*
>
> *But as many as received him, to them gave he power to become the sons of God, even to them that believe on his name:*
>
> *Which were born, not of blood, nor of the will of the flesh, nor of the will of man, but of God.*
>
> *And the Word was made flesh, and dwelt among us (and we beheld his glory, the glory as of the only begotten of the father), full of grace and truth.*'

The corporal reached for the latch and went out backwards. He shuffled through the snow, heedless of his way, like a drunken man, while wave upon wave of grief and nausea passed over him. But he could not weep; a rigid and hard power kept him going, and wakeful. He could have repeated the cobbler's last reading almost word for word; but it sounded only in his ear, not in his heart. So he lay down upon his bed, staring rigidly at the ceiling with his mind almost empty of thought, in bitter and savage self-defence, while all the time hunger raged in his stomach. When at last something like sleep sank upon him, it was not sound sleep; as indeed on that Christmas Eve only few of the prisoners seemed to sleep sound. Again and again the corporal started up, when the thin cover of his dreams was torn apart, even when one of his nearby companions coughed loudly, or turned over, or moaned. Once he was wakened by someone coming up to him, touching him on his shoulder, and pressing something into his hand. When he wakened he was just in time to see the cobbler going out. And then he felt a piece of bread in his hand. Greedily he began to eat.

Chapter Ten

JANUARY PASSED; slowly, tormentingly slowly. With February came frightful cold which made every day a torture. Then came March, and still the severe winter persisted. April came, and the men heard that they would be another two years in Russia. Two years longer they had to carry the burden which it was painful enough to drag from one day to the next.

Prisoner-of-War Fritz Becklam, in the three months since that Christmas Eve, had undergone a terrible change. It was as though he were wrapped in an evil, wilful, sick dream, which made a continual and ever more malicious mockery of him. There was scarcely anyone left who took him seriously. At best people were sorry for him, as he stumped about the camp on legs which had become thin and shaky, always freezing, with wild and staring looks, and pinched, defiant mouth, his haggard cheeks in a constant motion of chewing. He was no longer the ' penguin '; he looked more like a plucked stork or hawk. He had removed his moustache, too, by order of the Jewish doctor, and for a long time he had worn the same dirty winter clothes as all the rest; his emaciated and wrinkled neck rose up out of the thick collar of the steppe-jacket. He was tormented by hunger no less than all his companions. But he kept it to himself, sullen and defiant, although sometimes at night, on his bed, he would involuntarily grind his teeth. If he met one of the cooks he lowered his glance or looked away, in order not to beg, when perhaps he would have been given something. For the cooks, who were not so hard driven by hunger, were still the likeliest people to have Becklam repeat his stories. He did not go to them. He had his 'pride'. Nor did he go to the cobbler. To make up for this, however, Ewald Mette had come to him several times late at night, and like a figure in a dream, had passed a piece of bread into his hand, which Becklam had greedily swallowed.

Fritz Becklam had fallen silent, in a horrible, tortured way, just as if his evil spirit, which had driven him so long into false speech, had now robbed him of speech, which might have been able to free him and open a way back for him into life with his fellow-men. Only very seldom, as he stood with his companions, freezing in a corner of the working site, or sitting with them round a quickly kindled secret fire, seeking protection from the cruel cold—very seldom, on such occasions, did it happen that one or other would mockingly say to the corporal: 'Well, Fritz, when are we getting home now? You know the date?'

Then there would burst forth from him as from a man possessed: 'You will see that we get home! You will see, you fools!'

'Yes, but when? When?' asked one of the wags

again. 'You said that we should get home by Christmas time.'

'By Christmas?' cried the corporal. 'Nobody spoke of Christmas. She said, "by the great festival".'

'Who said?' asked some of them, who were not quite sure who was meant.

'His pretty little prophetess,' said the other, laughing. 'But, Fritz, man,' they turned to the corporal again, 'what great festival, then, are you talking about now?'

'What festival could it be, you stupid fools?' replied the corporal wrathfully. 'It's Easter, what else could it be?'

'The devil! Then we get home at Easter? But that's in a week, Becklam!'

'Of course it is.' The corporal stretched his thin neck like a sick vulture and compressed his lips frantically, as though he had to keep his last secret to himself in face of these scoffers. 'Of course we are now getting home!'

'We? All of us?' they wanted to know.

'That depends on yourselves.'

'How? I thought it depended on your thumb nail?'

'Leave my thumb nail out of it. That's quite true, anyway. She said that when the nail is white again and the great festival comes——'

'Then we'll get home!' interrupted the wags. 'Three cheers for Becklam! But what if you've taken us in again?'

'It depends on yourselves. I at least am going home at Easter, you'll see that all right!'

'You are? In a one-man transport, I suppose? My

dear chap,' added his companions, changing their tone, ' my dear chap, don't talk rubbish.'

' I am going home at Easter,' repeated the corporal solemnly, looking round the circle fanatically, and again compressing his lips in that tell-tale way.

' Fritz, Fritz,' the others said, in an effort to talk him over, ' it's a long way, and the nights are cold. You're as weak as water. Don't be mad, Fritz! '

But he only went on saying that he would begin the journey home at Easter. For so far everything that had been prophesied had come to pass, even if he had mis-understood a great deal—as, for example, concerning his brother's death. For Maria had only said that Albert would at such and such a time be ' free '. Of course she meant by that his death, unfortunately; for every-thing happens as it is determined, and nothing can be changed. And so with the journey home everything would happen absolutely as foretold. Everyone would see it, especially those who now thought that they could make merry over such serious matters.

' Fritz, you're spinning a yarn! ' said the good-natured ones. ' You've got a bee in your bonnet, and you're going crazy. Come, be a man! '

But he had befooled himself much too deeply; it was no longer possible to speak to him. It even became clear that every attempt to make the unhappy man see reason only strengthened him in his aberration, so that finally the others looked on him as they would a madman, and let him be. When, later, some of them tried to bring him to his senses by recalling to him his brother's fate, then their failure was all the greater. For scarcely was the name of Albert uttered than the corporal made the bitterest accusations against his brother. In him could be seen how a man may be so stubborn and crazy that he ceases to see what it is that matters in life; that he ' loses courage and faith ', and that he awaits death like an old woman. But he would . . . and once again he presumptuously boasted, in his sullen and arrogant spirit, that he would fulfil the prophecy. At Easter he would go home. That was as true ' as the Amen in church '.

' Just watch him ! ' said his comrades, who heard this remark with serious faces. ' The man's ready for anything now. He's no longer responsible for his actions.'

Chapter Eleven

IN FACT, during the next few days, the corporal could be seen, both in the camp and outside at the fenced labour sites, roaming near the barbed wire, and slinking round the camp gates, with an expression of mingled cunning and resolution. About a week before Easter he was put into a very large working-party which was at work outside the town, on a building site which could not be easily guarded. Russians and Germans mingled here during working hours. The enormous area of the site was surrounded by a cordon of guards who had, however, only a rough view of the whole.

It was Good Friday and an ordinary working day. But the German prisoners who were working in the town had already spoken in the camp of how the approach of Easter was to be felt everywhere. The Russians had not forgotten this festival which had once been the most sacred of all for them; they cleaned and decorated their houses, they had even baked something resembling cakes. It almost seemed as though here, too, on the great bare building site with its half-finished and already half-decayed new buildings, its stalls and shops and lavatories and ditches, its drainage pipes and cranes, a kind of hidden and restless joy had taken possession of people—against every rule and regulation—for there was more activity, more traffic, more bustle to be noticed than at any other time. The Russian workers crowded in front of the shops, stood around chatting, and surged hither and thither. In consequence it was by no means so difficult for an individual to disappear among the Russians who streamed in and out, especially since there was little external difference between them and the prisoners. Germans and Russians wore the same dirty, padded clothes, the same fur caps; nor did the Russians after that severe winter look any less starved than the Germans.

When that evening the N.C.O. in charge of the guard counted the working-party which was filed up ready for the march back to camp, one man was missing. This misfortune befell, of all people, a sergeant who had always treated the prisoners decently and reasonably, who gave them such liberties as were possible, and was therefore thoroughly liked by the Germans. Now the decent Ukrainian peasant lad ran up and down the rows cursing and counting at the same time. Everyone knew that those in charge of the guard were severely punished if prisoners were missing; and every prisoner would gladly have spared this young sergeant any unpleasantness, in order that he might not become embittered and disillusioned.

But no counting was of any avail; one man was missing, and soon everyone knew that it was Fritz Becklam. Many had indeed seen this coming. For two whole hours the men had to wait in their ranks in the cold.

The Russian picket officer and an NKVD man with him came from the camp to learn the facts; the leader of the corporal's brigade was threatened with punishment. Were the men in the working-party to be blamed for being bitter and furious when they thought of the man who had played them this trick? Every normal man knew that such a flight was senseless. In two days at the outside the idiot would be caught and would get a sound thrashing. Nor would the camp guards be specially delighted to have to tear through the district day and night, hunting for such a wild fool.

In the meantime, however, it was only P.O.W. Corporal Fritz Becklam who was tearing through the district. He really was tearing. He was tearing like a man gone amok.

After he had succeeded in passing through the cordon of guards in the midst of a fairly large company of Russians, he was seized with a feeling of mad triumph. He was free, he had begun his journey home! Now the doubters and mockers would see whether or not his prophecy was fulfilled. And he plunged on into the twilight, panting, his legs trembling and his heart thumping in his throat, but with the incomprehensible strength of a fanatic or a madman. The sun set; he raced after it, for where it set was the goal and end of his journey. Even when darkness had completely fallen he did not cease his mad race. With the instinct of the old soldier, of the hunted animal, he knew that the first hours were decisive. Before morning came he had to be far away, and to have found a good hiding-place in this bare, endlessly flat country. Then later he had to try and make use of a goods train. But first he must get so far away from the camp that the guards lost the desire to follow him further!

Towards morning he approached a wood, at its edge a great barn packed to the roof with straw. He hid himself so cunningly and laboriously that the Russians would have to search the whole enormous mass of straw if they were to find him. And when he had crept in and hidden, he suddenly felt as though he had become quite tiny in his great straw mountain. How fine it was! He had ceased to exist, he was invisible, he could not be found. Nothing more could torment him, no camp, no fear, no hunger, no Russians, nothing, nothing.

But at last hunger wakened him. He felt the cold, too, even though he was so deep in the straw. But the hunger was worse. It must be broad daylight, perhaps midday. Heavens, how hungry he was! He began to chew straw. Then he listened. Nothing. Not a sound. It was best for him to remain hidden till the evening. But how painfully slowly the hours went by! It was like eternity. At any moment they could come upon him. What would they do with him? Should he peep out? No, no! Not yet. He was so weak and feeble that he could scarcely move his limbs. But that was all one, for he was on the way home. It was almost as though he sat in the train and the wheels were rattling over the lines . . . rat-a-tat . . . rat-a-tat . . . rat-a-tat. From time to time he lapsed into a light half-sleep; then the train really was carrying him home. And at home they were preparing to welcome him. They were standing at the door, mother with her silk apron, his sister, and Karl, the eldest brother. There was a smell of seed cake. 'But where is Albert?' asked his mother. 'Albert? Oh, blow Albert! He wouldn't listen to reason. He lost his firm faith.' Then the old woman shook her head. 'Well, so long as you are here, Fritz. Come, eat and drink! But Albert—didn't you hold him by the hand?'

At last his hunger was unbearable. It could not go on like that, even if he had to risk everything. Laboriously he burrowed his way out of the straw. . . . Evening had really come again. And they had not caught him. It was not ordained that he should be caught. He would go on. He would also get food. Cautiously he slid down from the heap of straw to the ground. But he collapsed there immediately, his legs were so weak. Never mind. He did not remain lying, but with clenched teeth he stood up and slunk towards the wood, behind which the tired winter sun had just set. It was a poor, thin little wood, the crossing of which offered no difficulty. After the wood came more open land. Here more care was needed. Again and again he stopped behind some thorny bush, and bending low looked all around. The night was huge and indifferent above him. Not a star in the sky, that was good. If only the pangs of hunger did not rage so in his intestines! It was as though firebrands were running through him from his stomach. Now it was settled: at the next house he would get food.

But no house came. Field upon field, nothing but fields. How could there be so many fields together! A village must come in the end. How cruel this earth in Russia was! Damp, heavy, boggy, it clung to him, Every step was a torment, each separate step. At last the ground grew firmer, there were bushes and trees. And then, after an eternity, a house loomed before him, he was not deceived, there were even several houses. He had no will or sensations left; everything had ceased to matter. He reeled in at the first door he came upon.

A large, low room, feebly lit by an oil-lamp. In the middle of the room stood an old woman with a chamber-pot in her hand, who gave a cry of astonishment, not fear, when the stranger entered. Beneath the dark kerchief she had round her head her thick brows rose a little, and she puckered her mouth, which increased the innumerable friendly wrinkles of her face. Then she shook her head, put the chamber-pot down in the middle of the room and approached the corporal.

'Well?' she said in Russian.

The fugitive leaned against the wall beside the door, his arms dangling.

'Give me something to eat, mother,' he said with his last strength. *'Daj kuschatj, matka.'*

'Oh, a German!' exclaimed the old woman in astonishment, but again without fear. And when she had examined the weak and broken intruder more closely, great pity appeared on her face. And then she said simply: 'Come, sit down, German, sit down!'

The corporal tried to walk to the table, further in the room; but his knees gave way at the second step. The old woman said something cross and gruff, as though she were scolding a naughty child; then she grasped the man resolutely under his arms and dragged him to the table. She brought bread from a corner, put down some milk, some pea soup, firm and fatty, then: 'Eat, lad!' was all she said.

The corporal gulped down everything which the old woman set before him. But he did not enjoy it; he felt like a stray dog which had made off somewhere with a stolen bone. What would happen now? The old woman had, of course, realized at once what he was: these Russians were cleverer than one gave them credit for. Would she summon help in order to capture him? Did she only give him something to eat so that he should not run away at once? But the old woman had ceased to trouble about the stranger; she was playing with a little child which was sitting on the floor in a corner. Only when she noticed that the German had finished eating did she sit down again beside him and look at him; and after she had looked at him for a long time she sighed softly and crossed herself.

'She is religious!' the thought flashed through the fugitive's mind. 'That's good!' And all at once it did him good to look at her dear, strong face. His fears were scattered; there fell upon him a kind of gentle swoon, a kind of sleep and pleasant dream. For a few moments he again thought that his own mother was before him. And the quiet, strange dialogue of the returned son was resumed with the old woman. Once more he had to justify himself in respect of his dead brother; but the old woman did not condemn him. She loved him, she forgave him. . . . Oh, how good that was, how good!

116

'Come, German,' said the old Russian. 'Lie down and sleep.'

She again took him under his arms, propped him up like a drunken man, and when at last he was on his feet, she pointed to the enormous tiled stove placed along the long wall of the room. 'There, lie down,' she commanded him. '*Itti spatj!*'

Painfully the corporal clambered on to the stove. It was gloriously warm up there, and soft with many furs and blankets. Heavens, how it did one good to lie here! As his senses left him he saw an old man and a young girl entering; both looked at him in astonishment, then he sank into good and deep darkness. . . .

In his dreams he heard a lovely song which came out of a great depth and swelled up to him, ever nearer, ever stronger. He wakened and could not believe his eyes: from the top of the stove he saw at least fifteen or twenty people gathered in the room. They were all kneeling in a semi-circle in front of an illuminated ikon in one corner of the room; the candles cast a warm glow over it (so that Becklam could half see the image of a noble form, enthroned), as the kneeling figures looked up devoutly to the object of their adoration. At the same time they were singing a song of many parts, which flowed and ebbed like peaceful, friendly waves. The room was filled with these waves, which seemed to come from a great and holy distance.

'Easter,' thought the corporal. 'They are still religious. They are celebrating Easter!' That lessened his danger. Perhaps it was best to remain lying where he was. Perhaps they were all Russians like Maria or

Nina; they would not betray him. The old woman would certainly not. Besides, he was still so weak that he could not move. No, it had to be all right. So long as he lay still, lay still, and kept a good watch. . . . And it was fine to be submerged in this sea of prayer and song. How festive the whole room suddenly was, almost like Christmas Eve at home. And while the fugitive listened and gazed, without thinking, he felt himself absorbed more and more in a still and shining peace, such as he had not felt for a long time, perhaps had never felt before. . . . He could not understand it. And the light shone in his sleep and made him still. . . .

When he wakened again, the room was empty. The lights were still burning in front of the ikon, but the night was already yielding to the murky day. He heard someone stir beside him, and the sound of soft breathing. A young woman lay beside him, and behind her an elderly man. The two were sleeping deeply and soundly beside the stranger, as if it had always been so. In the bed below he saw the old woman's face on the pillows, the little child beside her.

But this could not go on. He could not stay where he was now that day was breaking. The corporal crept down from his resting-place. He felt refreshed, even though he was still weak. On the table there was a loaf of bread. He cut himself a slice and swallowed it greedily. Once again he looked round the dimly lit room, which was as wretched as a cow-shed, but also as warm and as homely. He would have given a lot to have been able to stay there—for ever, if need be, as a man among men.

He slunk out cautiously, and went on his way. When it was broad daylight, a few young lads suddenly encountered him at a place where the road went through a narrow cutting. They laughed when they saw him, and shouted, 'German! German!' They held him fast, gave him bread to eat and spirits to drink. But they still held him fast; laughing and joking, they took him with them, in spite of his resistance. In the next village they shut him up in a room and gave him a good meal; all the time laughing and joking. After a few hours had elapsed he was taken away by the militia and returned to his camp. Just short of the camp his own guards took him over and thrashed him.

The journey was over.

Chapter Twelve

SOME DAYS LATER a man came running to Ewald Mette, the cobbler, in his workshop, and shouted: 'Ewald, Ewald, come out! They're beating your prophet to death!'

The cobbler left everything lying and hastily ran after the man.

He had wanted to befriend the corporal after he had been returned to the camp, but the corporal's attitude made it clear that he did not want to have anything to do with anyone. Most of the prisoners of war were openly hostile to the unhappy man, after his last escapade. They had not forgotten that on his account they had frozen for two hours and had alienated a good sergeant of the guard. At first, when he was brought back to the camp, pitifully beaten and starved, they were still able to be sorry for him. But after a few days they began to knock him around and to abuse him whenever they saw him. The corporal took it all in silence. He had become very quiet. This silent and patient endurance was regarded by the embittered men as shameless and crazy insolence. If he had said: 'I see now, friends, that I've been stupid. Forgive me,' perhaps they would have left him in peace, as he was so clearly 'all in'. But he did not do this. He was still too broken up, too much concerned with himself, after all that he had gone through. He was in a ferment. And now on some trivial occasion a few of them, whom hunger and homesickness had deprived of their self-control, began to beat up the corporal in the hut.

The corporal had once been a good soldier, he was no coward or milksop, not even now. He defended himself, hit back. But since he had no strength left, and was only just able to keep on his feet, he was very quickly worsted; it was not long before his opponents had him on the ground and were beating him and stamping on him. It looked as though they meant to finish him off.

Mette the cobbler rushed into the hut, his face a fiery red, his eyes staring from his head. In a voice shaking with fury, which had lost every trace of its country calm, he shouted at the raging men, and wrenched apart the little group of sadistic onlookers. The frenzy immediately left Becklam's assailants, and they drew off.

'Are you still men?' roared the cobbler. His round head jerked forward from his heavy shoulders, like a tortoise's head coming out of its shell. The men, suddenly sobered, looked round the circle, patted and pulled at their clothes. 'It's all he deserved,' came a voice from the circle of onlookers.

And one of the assailants, white with excitement, stared at the cobbler, and exclaimed: 'No, we're not men any more. But that tale-spinner there is to blame!'

'Oh, you ——!' shouted the cobbler at the circle.

'So long as you have someone of whom you can say: "He is to blame! Kill him!" that has always been the simplest way! But that you have made him like this with your impatience and your unbelief and your curiosity—and—and——' He swallowed and coughed and then went on: 'You don't like to hear that, do you? Who was it who wanted to hear that godless twaddle? It wasn't you, I suppose? Who was it who swallowed the words whole out of the poor devil's mouth? Not you, I suppose? Oh, you damned hypocrites, if you could just see your own ugly mugs, you miserable creatures! Come on, get a hold of him!' he said to the man standing nearest to him.

The corporal lay as though dead. His right eye was very swollen and bloodshot. Blood was streaming from his nose, over his mouth and down his chin. When they lifted him up he moaned heavily and painfully.

'Take him to my hut!' ordered the cobbler, his voice still shaking with fury. None of the men had ever seen him so agitated. No one dared to say a word: they all fell back, abashed, one of them held the door open, and a good many went with the wretched little procession the few steps from the hut to the cobbler's quarters.

When they had laid the corporal on the cobbler's bed, Mette immediately bundled all the inquisitive men out of the room, and said to the man who had helped him to carry the corporal: 'Fetch the doctor! Quickly!'

Then he took his towel, damped it under the tap, came back to Fritz Becklam and washed his blood-stained face. As he did this he spoke incessantly, in his indescribable excitement, both to himself and to the humiliated man.

'Just see,' he said, and his kind, country voice trembled, sounding in his agitation much more Saxon than usual, 'just see what's become of you, you silly ass. You wanted to be like God, you exalted yourself above men, and what are you now, you poor creature? Where has your evil spirit landed you? You can be happy that it hasn't strangled you completely and thrown you on the midden like a sick cockerel!'

With his skilful cobbler's hands he wiped Becklam's face clean, now here, now there, for the blood was still streaming. 'But don't take it into your head to die now, you poor chump!' he said. 'Or to take leave like the fox from the dovecote! If you do that, you'll catch it! You'll catch it from Ewald Mette! No, no, my dear fellow, you'll open your eyes at last. You will change. You will ask forgiveness of God and of men. You're going to *live*! Ah-ha, my friend, you don't get away so easily by the back door. No, no, my dear chap. Life is much too serious for that. Your brother—yes, your brother, he could die. He had got as far as that. But you are just at the beginning, at the very beginning. Do you understand, or not?'

The corporal gave a deep moan. He opened his eyes, looked at the cobbler. The cobbler covered up the bleeding eye with his towel. But he gazed furiously into the corporal's sound open eye, almost choking in his terrible agitation. 'Listen, Fritz,' he exclaimed. 'Listen to me! Are you listening? You don't get away with it like that. You'll stay right here and take it upon

123

yourself. Everything, the shame, the need, the burden, the cross. You'll be a man and not something else, you stupid pig. And if you take it upon yourself, as is the proper thing to do, just as I do, and everybody else, then it'll be all right with you, too, whether you go home or rot in Russia! Are you listening, did you hear me, man?'

The corporal closed his sound eye for a while. After a time he opened it again and looked at the voluble cobbler, as though meaning to say: 'Go on speaking, go on.'